DIAGNOSIS:
EXPECTING BOSS'S BABY
Jacqueline Diamond

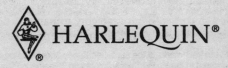

TORONTO • NEW YORK • LONDON
AMSTERDAM • PARIS • SYDNEY • HAMBURG
STOCKHOLM • ATHENS • TOKYO • MILAN • MADRID
PRAGUE • WARSAW • BUDAPEST • AUCKLAND

Special thanks to Marcia Holman,
who provided her nursing expertise

ISBN 0-373-16962-0

DIAGNOSIS: EXPECTING BOSS'S BABY

Printed in U.S.A.

"Dr. Rourke asked me to drop off some prenatal vitamins for Natalie.

"I was downstairs at the lab, so I just popped up."

"I'm sorry?" Patrick couldn't make sense of the nurse's explanation. Why would Natalie be collecting someone else's prenatal vitamins?

"We didn't have any when she came in."

"When she came in?" he repeated, feeling as if he'd missed some vital point.

It was six weeks since he'd made love to Natalie. And he had used protection.

Natalie might have consulted with Dr. Rourke for a routine physical. But there was no reason for the obstetrician to send over prenatal vitamins unless…

…his secretary was pregnant.

Special deliveries straight to the heart!

Diagnosis: Expecting Boss's Baby
(HAR #962, 3/03)

Prescription: Marry Her Immediately
(HAR #971, 5/03)

Prognosis: A Baby? Maybe
(HAR #978, 7/03)

Dear Reader,

This month we have a wonderful lineup of stories, guaranteed to warm you on these last chilly days of winter. First, Charlotte Douglas kicks things off with *Surprise Inheritance*, the third installment in Harlequin American Romance's MILLIONAIRE, MONTANA series, in which a sexy sheriff is reunited with the woman he's always loved when she returns to town to claim her inheritance.

Next, THE BABIES OF DOCTORS CIRCLE, Jacqueline Diamond's new miniseries centered around a maternity and well-baby clinic, premieres this month with *Diagnosis: Expecting Boss's Baby*. In this sparkling story, an unforgettable night of passion between a secretary and her handsome employer leads to an unexpected pregnancy.

Also available this month is *Sweeping the Bride Away* by Michele Dunaway. A bride-to-be is all set to wed "Mr. Boring" until she hires a rugged contractor who makes her pulse race and gives her second thoughts about her upcoming nuptials. Rounding things out is *Professor & the Pregnant Nanny* by Emily Dalton. This heartwarming story pairs a single dad in need of a nanny for his three adorable children with a woman who is alone, pregnant and in need of a job.

Enjoy this month's offerings as Harlequin American Romance continues to celebrate twenty years of publishing the best in contemporary category romance fiction. Be sure to come back next month for more stories guaranteed to touch your heart!

Melissa Jeglinski
Associate Senior Editor
Harlequin American Romance

ABOUT THE AUTHOR

Jacqueline Diamond comes from a long line of babies. In addition, her father was the doctor who delivered her. At the time, he was a country doctor in Menard, Texas, and later went on to become a psychiatrist in Louisville, Kentucky, and Nashville, Tennessee. Jackie now lives in Orange County, California, with her husband, two sons and two formerly stray cats. You can write to Jackie at P.O. Box 1315, Brea, CA 92822, or by e-mail at JDiamondfriends@aol.com.

Books by Jacqueline Diamond

HARLEQUIN AMERICAN ROMANCE

HARLEQUIN INTRIGUE

*The Babies of Doctors Circle

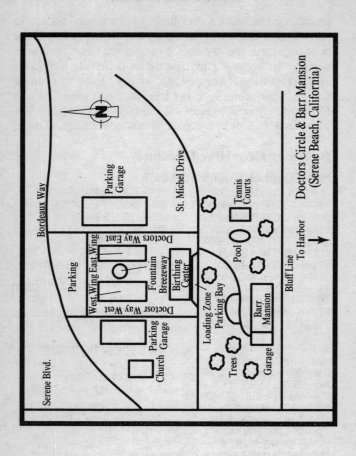

Doctors Circle & Barr Mansion
(Serene Beach, California)

Chapter One

Natalie Winford knew she had just made the biggest mistake of her life. She didn't regret a minute of it.

Rum punch, she thought. They could both blame it on the rum punch, if they had to blame it on anything.

Outside, she heard the harbor water slap lightly at the yacht. Here in the master cabin, a stray sunbeam through the porthole burnished Patrick Barr's tanned skin to molten gold as he lay amid the tangled sheets.

Natalie never wanted to move again. She yearned to lie forever in Patrick's arms, suspended in this magic interval after making love.

"Nat?" he murmured.

"Right here." At such close range, she was acutely aware of the man's lime-scented cologne and the well-proportioned build that testified to his high-school and college days as a competitive diver. Playfully she ran her hand across the muscles of his shoulders and back, relishing their sculpted power.

Until now, she'd only been able to dream about touching him. For five years, she'd answered his phone calls, sorted his mail, scheduled his appointments and fantasized about him from a distance. Until today.

When Patrick first took over as administrator of the

Doctors Circle Clinic and Birthing Center from his disorganized predecessor, Natalie had been relieved to work for a man she respected. Over the years, her feelings had developed into intense admiration.

Now she drank in every detail of the man in bed beside her. She treasured his strong, sensitive nose and the two pucker lines between his intelligent brown eyes. She cherished his thick brown hair, although it was a little too long because, as usual, he'd been too busy to stop by a barbershop.

Patrick seemed to be making his own assessment of Natalie, she noticed as his gaze trailed from her breasts up to her soft lips. "You always look terrific, but the view is even better without clothes," he said. After a moment's reflection, he added ruefully, "On the other hand, I'm afraid we jumped into this situation without thinking."

"If you're about to say you wish we hadn't done this, I'll kick you out of bed," Natalie said.

He flashed a warm, masculine smile. "I couldn't possibly regret it. But…"

"I know." She sighed. "My behavior hardly meets your high standards."

Patrick ran his hand through his already rumpled hair. "You haven't done anything wrong. I'm the one who needs to set a good example for the community."

Until she met her boss, Natalie hadn't known anyone could be so hard on himself or so exacting with his staff. She wished she'd been raised with the same insistence on honesty and integrity, but not everyone had the advantage of two stable parents with high ideals.

In any case, making love with Patrick didn't break the rules as far as Natalie was concerned. A twenty-nine-year-old woman had a right to find happiness with a single man, even if they were boss and secretary. And even if it might only last one afternoon.

"You did set a good example today, during the cruise," she said. "The community loved what you said about Doctors Circle's future plans. That's why the pledges came rolling in."

The luncheon outing aboard Patrick's yacht had launched a nine-month-long Endowment Fund drive aimed at raising thirty million dollars, enough to put Doctors Circle on firm financial footing for years to come. The movers and shakers of Serene Beach, California, had responded by opening their checkbooks.

Most of them were aware that the yacht, *Melissa,* was named after the infant sister Patrick never knew. It was her loss from lung problems and prematurity that had inspired his parents, once they overcame poverty and rose to prominence in the business community, to establish a center to save other babies.

After the guests and crew left, Natalie and Patrick had sat on deck toasting their success with rum punch. They'd been exhilarated, energized and intensely attuned to each other after weeks of working twelve-hour days together.

She didn't know what had finally overcome their inhibitions, and she didn't care. She just wanted to stay here in his cabin forever and forget that the rest of the world existed.

"It was a great kickoff, thanks in large part to you." Patrick stretched lazily. Although the August sun lingered outside, it was past seven o'clock.

"If only they could see you now." Teasingly, Natalie traced a finger down the center of his chest. "On second thought, I'd rather keep you to myself."

"You're in a wonderful mood," he said.

"You ought to be, too."

"I am." He pulled her tighter against him. "You know, I just got a terrific idea."

"For the next fund-raiser?" Natalie asked.

"Something a little more personal." Angling toward her, Patrick cupped the back of her head with his hand. He scanned her face as if trying to memorize every detail, and then his mouth claimed hers.

His kiss exploded with yearning. Natalie melted against him, yielding to his tongue's demands and savoring the sensation of being held close.

When Patrick lifted his head, she kissed the V of his collarbone. "I think I figured out your idea."

"Do you approve?"

"Utterly," she said.

He reached into a drawer for more protection, and then he pushed her gently down against the sheet.

NATALIE AWOKE in darkness, filled with dismay. Her subconscious mind had finally registered what they'd done, and the likelihood that it would lead to disaster.

Patrick slept on his back, with one hand resting on her shoulder. Natalie brushed her cheek against it.

She knew his hands well. They were large hands, capable of carving the air in an expansive gesture or dashing his name across a document that granted medical services to a poor woman.

And her hands? They'd served plenty of hamburgers while she made her way through high school. They'd also signed a marriage license with a man who turned out to be an alcoholic, and a few years later they'd signed the divorce papers.

Her hands had written something else, too, an entry on her job application that hadn't been completely hon-

est. Natalie shuddered to think that Patrick might someday find out.

Well, he wasn't going to. She'd let matters go way
too far tonight, but there was still time to run damage
control.

Quietly, she rose and dressed in her tailored slacks
and sailor-style blouse. With the brush from her purse,
she tucked her blond hair into its accustomed bun.

It was time to go, before Patrick awoke and realized
what a mistake this had been. Or, worse, failed to realize it. The better he got to know her, the more likely
it became that he would discover some unpleasant
truths.

There was only one course to follow. At work, Natalie would be all business, signaling Patrick to keep his
distance.

They'd pretend that their going to bed together never
happened. At least they could still work together, sharing the closeness they'd developed over these past five
years. And she'd hang on to her pride.

But she'd discovered a passion in herself that had
lain dormant all her days. Even when she was married,
she'd never felt more than passing pleasure. With Patrick, only with Patrick, did she truly come alive.

It hurt to know that she might never hold him again,
but that was all right. Natalie could bear it, as long as
she didn't lose him entirely.

ON MONDAY Patrick had a headache. He knew it was
partly from overindulging in rum punch the previous
day and partly from listening to the construction work
going on downstairs.

The East Wing, which housed the administration services and the radiology department, was one of three

structures that made up Doctors Circle, along with the Birthing Center and the West Wing office building. Downstairs in the East Wing, space formerly rented by an outside pediatric clinic was being converted into an infertility center.

Wham-wham-wham! went something that sounded like a pile driver, although Patrick couldn't imagine why such heavy equipment was needed. The pounding throbbed right through his brain.

He had a lot of work to do today, catching up on paperwork and planning for the next big fund-raising event, an Oktoberfest celebration. Yesterday's donations, while generous, paled before the amount of money needed to cushion the center against the sort of financial upheaval that had nearly swamped it a few years earlier.

Patrick fumbled in his drawer for an aspirin. No such luck. Wouldn't you know that in a medical office the last thing you could find was a simple pain remedy?

He punched the intercom. "Nat? Could you come in here, please?"

"Yes, sir," she replied crisply.

A moment later, Natalie entered his office. The breezy woman from the yacht had vanished. Today, her hair was pinned back and her body hidden beneath a trim navy-and-white suit with a red scarf at the throat.

Patrick peered at her blearily across his broad oak desk. At the moment, he was in no shape to try to renew their camaraderie. "I was hoping you had an aspirin," he managed to say. "I can't think straight."

"Sorry. I'm not authorized to dispense medication."

He insisted on strict rules, but not that strict. "You don't need an M.D. to hand out aspirin."

Natalie smiled. "That was a joke. Guess you're not in the mood, huh? Hold on, I'll get you some."

"Doesn't it bother you?" he asked. "I mean, World War III going on downstairs?"

"The assistant head of accounting and the chief radiologist came in to complain." Clearly, they hadn't fazed Natalie, who looked cool and collected as usual. "I reminded them that they used to beef about the noisy kids from the pediatric clinic. At least this is temporary. Hold on."

She ducked out, leaving an image of angelic freshness imprinted on Patrick's brain. Despite the fact that his head felt swollen to the size of a basketball, he took pleasure in his secretary's appearance.

For years he'd tried not to notice her bright blue eyes and lively face. Especially he'd struggled to ignore the figure that, despite the cloaking effect of her tailored suits, was nothing short of delicious.

Patrick had never expected to breach the unspoken barrier between director and employee. He knew himself, and getting involved with any woman, particularly one he worked with, was a losing proposition. It also appeared that he might be taking advantage of his position, something he had no intention of doing.

Yet their lovemaking had surpassed anything in his experience. Even with a blinding headache, he was ready—well, almost ready—for a rematch, if only he could figure out what to do about his aching morals.

The door squeaked as Natalie returned with two pills and a cup of water. "Here you go." She handed them over.

When their hands touched, an awareness of her heat and vibrancy pulsed through Patrick. Against his will, desire quickened his blood. "I feel better already."

"You haven't taken them yet."

"I don't really need to—" *Wham-wham-wham!* went the downstairs equipment, dispelling his objections. Up went the cup and down went the pills. "What on earth are they doing?" he asked when he could speak again.

"I think they're chipping away some tile," Natalie said.

Patrick should have known that, since he'd been involved in every step of the remodeling plans. But right now, with the sight of Natalie stirring male hormones into a frenzy, he couldn't recall much of anything.

He needed to find out how she felt. "About yesterday..." he began.

"I'm fine," she said. "Now, I'd better get back to my desk." She turned to leave.

"Nat!"

"Yes, sir?"

"First of all, stop calling me sir."

"Yes, Doctor," she said.

Patrick regarded her in confusion. He was much better at formulating goals and taking command than at reading people, especially the people closest to him. "We need to discuss where we stand."

Natalie took a deep breath, a movement that swelled her generous breasts. Patrick's hands still retained an impression of their softness, centered by the stiff arousal of her nipples. Oh, he was sure in control of himself today, wasn't he, he thought wryly.

"I was hoping we wouldn't have to talk about last night," she said.

Patrick respected her privacy, but he felt he owed her. "Please, have a seat. If I offended you last night, I apologize."

"You didn't. Not at all." Natalie perched on the edge of an upholstered chair. "It was just as much my fault."

"I'm your employer, which makes the responsibility all mine."

"Look, Dr. Barr." She leveled her blue gaze at him, to devastating effect. He wanted her so much he could hardly breathe. "Let's pretend the incident never happened."

"What incident?"

"You and me...on the boat!" Natalie gave an angry little bounce on her chair.

"You're referring to our lovemaking as an incident?" For Patrick, the experience had been delirious. And, of course, a huge error in judgment.

"I'm being discreet," Natalie said. "Which is a quality we both lost on your boat, along with our clothes."

"I agree," he said reluctantly. "Nevertheless—"

"The point is, we're simply not suited to each other." Natalie had retreated behind a mask. "What happened was great, but it was a one-time thing."

Patrick knew he ought to feel relieved. Her practical attitude meant they could get on with their work, which was what mattered, but he was oddly reluctant to let her go. "We should discuss this over dinner."

"In this town, if we ate dinner together, everyone would be gabbing about it," Natalie said.

"We've eaten dinner together before," he said.

"In the cafeteria with stacks of files between us. That doesn't count." His secretary stood up. "Look, Dr. Barr, there's no point in arguing about it. Last night was—what do you call it?—an anomaly. Let's go back to the way things were. No hard feelings, okay?"

Patrick arose also. His headache had faded, so now he was thinking clearly.

He respected her obvious regret about their liaison. He, too, knew it hadn't been a good idea, even though a rebellious part of him desperately wanted to repeat the mistake. "You're sure about this?"

"Yes, Dr. Barr."

"I have one request," he said.

"What's that?" Natalie's eyes narrowed.

"Call me by my first name," Patrick said. "You haven't called me Dr. Barr since the first six months we worked together. People would wonder about it."

"Okay." She looked relieved that he hadn't asked anything more difficult. "Excuse me, I hear someone in the outer office. I'll go check."

She sounded like her old, cheerful self. Apparently she was glad he'd agreed not to pursue her.

Good. His brief insanity yesterday hadn't spoiled their friendship or their highly effective working relationship. The last thing he wanted was for anything to interfere with saving the medical center for which his father had given his life.

NATALIE HELD OPEN Patrick's door for Spencer Sorrell, chief of the Doctors Circle Well-Baby Clinic. Unlike the pediatric clinic that had vacated its offices downstairs and relocated to a new building down the street, his department was an official arm of the medical center, not merely a tenant.

He'd been grousing a lot lately, mostly about his contention that his department should get the newly remodeled offices. Spencer, who believed he should have become administrator, instead of Patrick, always found something to complain about.

He brushed by Natalie without a word, which didn't surprise her. The senior pediatrician rarely spoke to her, and when he did, it was in a clipped, impersonal manner, as if she were a robot.

Spencer's brother, Finn, was the town's chief of police. Finn knew way too much about Natalie's family and her past, and it appeared that he'd shared that information with Spencer.

Her cheeks burning, she sat behind her desk. She was angry at Spencer for his snobbery and angry at herself for caring.

Natalie knew better than anyone what an insignificant position she occupied in the social whirl of Serene Beach. That didn't mean she lacked pride, only that she saw the world as it was.

Well, she didn't aspire to high society, and she didn't feel inferior to anyone, either. She only wished she could erase a few parts of her past.

In particular, she wished she hadn't lied on her job application.

A MONTH LATER, on a Saturday morning, Natalie did something she hadn't done since she was a little girl. She threw up.

Aware that her period was overdue, she drove to a pharmacy for a pregnancy kit. At home she followed the directions, and a few minutes later found herself staring in disbelief at the pink test strip.

How was this possible? Patrick had used protection both times during their lovemaking.

Yet she knew from working around pregnant women that condoms weren't infallible. Sometimes they slipped or cracked. That must be what had happened, because she hadn't slept with another man since her divorce.

A sense of wonder softened Natalie's dismay. She was carrying Patrick's child, a wonderful little boy or girl who'd be smart and sweet and loving.

Then she caught sight of herself in the bathroom mirror. She looked almost exactly like a photo of her own mother as a young woman.

"You're me all over again," her mother used to say. But, as a teenager, Natalie had resolved that she would never, never repeat Angie's mistakes. Three deadbeat husbands, five children and an inability to keep a job had created a chaotic household and made Angie's kids outsiders at school.

Even when Natalie married an older man at the age of twenty-one, she'd been careful not to get pregnant right away. Her caution had been validated when, over the next three years, her husband, Ralph, began drinking, lost his job and ran up debts. He'd vanished, leaving his wife to pay them off.

She'd been working for a temp agency when she learned about the secretarial opening at Doctors Circle. Patrick's predecessor, Dr. Grier, had been tyrannical and grumpy, so there'd been frequent turnover in the position.

Knowing she had the right skills, Natalie had sailed into the interview with high hopes. It went well, too. She knew as soon as she met Dr. Grier—nicknamed Dr. Grief by the staff—that she could handle his moods.

Only when she began filling in the application did she discover that she didn't qualify on purely technical grounds. It seemed unfair and she desperately needed the salary and benefits. So she'd lied, and not just about one thing, either.

She still believed she'd made a wise choice. It was impossible to imagine her life without this job, without the staff at Doctors Circle who'd become like a family, and without Patrick.

Yet she was ashamed, too. Well, the heck with that! Natalie thought in a surge of defiance. Let other people walk a mile in her shoes before they passed judgment.

Restlessly she wandered into her living room, which was dominated by rabbits. There were china rabbits, stuffed rabbits, crocheted rabbits, plastic rabbits and even one rabbit said to be carved out of moon rock, although she doubted it. They crowded the shelves and several end tables.

Her collection had begun at the age of ten when her father gave her his one and only gift: a stuffed rabbit he'd won at a carnival ring toss. Two months later he'd disappeared from her life. Although she'd long ago outgrown her childish belief that the gift proved he loved her, images of rabbits still boosted her spirits.

She desperately needed a boost now. How would Patrick react to the news that he was going to be a father? Would his dark eyes glimmer with anticipation, or would he simply be shocked?

With his strong sense of honor, he'd probably feel obligated to marry her. Maybe, she hoped, he might even be glad for the excuse. But she had too much pride to marry Patrick without admitting what she'd done, and she knew what that would mean.

A few months ago he'd fired a lab technician for lying about his qualifications. He wouldn't tolerate deception, he'd said. Despite their close relationship, what were the odds he'd give Natalie a break?

If she leveled with him, she'd destroy everything: Patrick's trust, their future together, maybe even her ability to work for him.

She needed advice. The person to consult, she decided, was her friend Amy Ravenna, a patient counselor at Doctors Circle. Amy had good common sense and, at thirty-three, four more years of experience in life than Natalie did.

Picking up the phone, she dialed Amy's number. With luck, her friend's advice would prevent her from making some stupid mistake that might ruin everything.

Chapter Two

"Are those flowers for me?" Patrick's sister paused in the high-ceilinged foyer to sniff the elaborate arrangement. Her sweatpants and T-shirt were damp where they covered her swimsuit. "I don't suppose so, since you didn't know I was coming over."

Patrick finished knotting his tie in front of the hall mirror. "I'm afraid they aren't, but I knew you'd be here. You use the pool every Saturday."

"How'd you figure that out?" Bernie squawked. "Usually I swim and leave without bothering you. I figured you didn't know I was here."

"I can see the pool from my bedroom," Patrick reminded her. "Sis, I enjoy having you over, and the house is yours as much as mine."

"You bought out my half, remember?" She pushed back a curly strand of brown hair. "Honestly, I'm all grown up and married now. Mike and I have our own house. I just like to borrow the pool."

"Anytime." He meant it. Having grown up in the shadow of their older sister's stillbirth, Patrick had treasured the strong-willed baby who came along when he was four. There'd been times during his teens when he was embarrassed to be seen with his kid sis, but the two had become close over the years.

They'd comforted each other after their father's death five years ago, and again after their mother succumbed to cancer three years later. Bernie, a natural mother, liked to bring over casseroles, make sure Patrick kept healthy food in the refrigerator and examine the sprawling Barr mansion to make sure his latest housekeeper was properly cleaning the expanses of glass, tile and blond wood.

"So who's the lucky lady?" Bernie indicated the flowers again.

"Noreen McLanahan called in sick for today's luncheon." The event to honor volunteers, of whom Noreen was one of the most prominent, was scheduled for noon at the Serene Beach Yacht Club. "I figured a widow who lives alone could use some cheering up, so I'm going to visit her and give them to her."

It wasn't merely a matter of charity. Mrs. McLanahan, one of the center's biggest financial supporters and a member of its board of directors, was a peppery personality whose wry observations always kept Patrick laughing. He'd have treasured her even if she was penniless.

"You've got a kind heart for a grumpy old bachelor," Bernie said.

"Gee, thanks."

To his surprise, his sister wrapped her arms around him. Although tall and athletic, she only came to his shoulders. "Excuse me for being sentimental, but I'm proud of you."

"For taking flowers to a sick woman?" Patrick teased as Bernie stepped back, her cross-training shoes squeaking on the marble floor. ''I must be a real creep most of the time if you're impressed by this.''

''Yeah, right.'' His sister traced a finger along the front table. It came up clean, to her evident satisfaction. The last housekeeper, who'd lasted only six months, had left dust so thick Bernie could write notes in it, and did. ''The truth is, you make me feel guilty. I compensate by fussing over you.''

''Guilty? About what?''

''About my choosing to give up medical school to stay home and have kids while you're shepherding our family's legacy,'' she said.

''You made the best choice for you.'' Patrick adored his two young nephews. More than that, his sister's happy home served as an emotional anchor for him.

''What about your right to make choices? You never wanted to be an administrator, but you stepped up to bat when you saw the clinic falling apart,'' Bernie said.

''I just wish I'd done it sooner,'' Patrick said.

For as long as he could remember, he'd been fired by a sense of mission inspired by his older sister's still-birth. Initially, it had been his motivation for applying to medical school, but later he'd discovered he enjoyed practicing medicine for its own sake.

He'd been so caught up in his pediatric practice that he hadn't noticed the toll Doctors Circle was taking on his father. Even the Barr fortune, earned from Joe's invention of self-cleaning window glass, wasn't enough to underwrite all the center's charities and compensate for Dr. Grier's sloppy management. As chairman of the board, Joe had thrown himself into fund-raising with a frenzy, with the result that he dropped dead of a heart attack.

Patrick should have realized that the aging man was

pushing himself too hard. He should have given up his practice sooner to take on the administrative job.

He couldn't turn back the clock. He'd spent five years reorganizing the day-to-day operations and putting the budget on a sound footing, and now he was ensuring the future of Doctors Circle by establishing an Endowment Fund.

"No one could have forced Dad to slow down," Bernie said. "He was obsessed with the center, even more than Mom was. I know he was upset about their losing a child, but these things happen to lots of people."

"Dad didn't see it that way," Patrick said. "Did you know he blamed himself for Melissa's death?"

Bernie's face scrunched in surprise. "No! Why would he do that?"

"While Mom was pregnant, he spent all his time either at his janitorial job or out in the workshop, fiddling with his inventions," Patrick explained. "He told me that if he'd paid more attention, he'd have seen how she was suffering and insisted on better care."

"They couldn't afford it," Bernie said.

"He'd have borrowed the money if he had to." Patrick could still see the lines of pain etched in Joe Barr's face as he'd made this confession. Melissa's stillbirth had been fresh in the aging man's memory, even though decades had passed since the unhappy event.

How ironic that Joe had pulled himself out of poverty, gaining a fortune from marketing his self-cleaning glass, yet had never really enjoyed the money. He'd poured much of it into Doctors Circle, which he'd established fifteen years ago. For Patrick's father, it had been both a form of atonement and a sacred obligation.

"I wish I'd known so I could have set him straight,"

Bernie said. "Problems with the placenta can't always be corrected, even now. Mom never blamed him."

"I guess when we feel guilty, logic has nothing to do with it," Patrick said.

"Are you speaking of yourself?" she asked.

"Me?"

"Well, you're the one driving yourself like a maniac for the Endowment Fund," she said. "It won't bring Dad back."

"Thanks for trying to make me feel better," he said. "The truth is, I enjoy my work."

"You used to whistle more when you were in pediatrics." Bernie straightened a large, modern canvas that faced the curving staircase.

"I whistled?" Patrick didn't recall that particular habit.

"You also told more jokes," his sister said.

"I collected jokes to make my patients laugh," he protested. He'd loved working in pediatrics, but what he was doing now was crucial. "Sis, I've got to get going. I want to allow plenty of time to visit with Mrs. McLanahan."

"Don't let me stop you. I'm leaving, too. There's a pot of orange-glazed chicken in the refrigerator, by the way," Bernie said. "You can eat it tonight or tomorrow." With a wave, she went out the front door.

Patrick locked up, then carried the flowers to his car and set them on the rear seat. He eased the finely tooled sedan along the driveway, past the glistening pool.

He stole a glimpse at the high bluffs. The rear of the estate provided a spectacular view of Serene Beach and its harbor. Far below, September sunlight played over a butterfly swarm of sails.

The driveway curved left, away from the view. Patrick stopped at the estate's ironwork arch and waited for traffic to clear on St. Michel Drive.

In his childhood, this street had been little used. That was before the two-story medical buildings had sprung up on the far side, with their white stucco exteriors and red-tile roofs.

The family had built Doctors Circle on the land where an orange grove once stood, situated so that the back entrance to the Birthing Center faced the front of their estate. As a result, Patrick didn't have to commute far to his office.

Seeing no more cars, he turned right and drove the few blocks to Mrs. McLanahan's home. To his disappointment, the houseman reported she was sleeping. Patrick left the flowers with a note wishing her a speedy recovery.

He had plenty of time before the luncheon. All dressed up and nowhere to go. It was a rarity not to have every minute committed, and against his better judgment, he knew what he wanted to do.

It would be childish to head inland toward Natalie's apartment. For heaven's sake, he had almost no chance of glimpsing her unless he parked and rang her doorbell, which he wasn't going to do.

This past month, he'd watched for any indication that she hadn't meant it when she pushed him away. Like an inviting smile, a touch on the shoulder, a mention of their night together.

There hadn't been any. He kept telling himself it was for the best, yet he missed their closeness with an unaccustomed ache.

He was better off alone, though. Work absorbed and energized Patrick, and relationships only interfered.

Both of his previous involvements had failed miserably. During his internship, a girlfriend had broken off with him because of his inattention. Years later, a lawyer he'd dated had also called it quits, citing his long hours and frequent cancelations of their plans. She'd told him she hoped he never had children, because he'd make a lousy father.

She was right. Much as Patrick enjoyed being around kids, his work came first, and always would.

Natalie was right to keep him at arm's length. Patrick certainly didn't want to lose her the way he'd lost the other two women. But like a teenager with a crush, he was going to cruise by her place in the hope of catching an unguarded glimpse of her. A man was allowed the occasional bit of foolishness as long as it did no harm, he told himself.

He drove inland to the flat mesa area of Serene Beach. Palm trees, azaleas and calla lilies dressed up the modest homes and apartments.

Along the sidewalks clattered kids on tricycles and preteens on skateboards. Patrick drove cautiously, remembering from his emergency-room rotations what could happen when children darted into the street.

The fourplex where Natalie lived lay in the middle of a block. Patrick had dropped her off once when her car was in the shop, and he'd never forgotten the location.

A rental van stood double-parked in front of the building. As he swung past, he saw stacks of furniture through the open rear door, from which someone had lowered a ramp. Obviously these amateurs didn't realize or perhaps didn't care that they were blocking several cars.

At the next corner, Patrick made a U-turn and swung

back. This time, he spotted Natalie's small green hatchback at the curb, hemmed in by the truck.

What now? He had time to kill and a strong desire to see her. Irresolutely, he parked across the street and sat considering his options.

Before he could decide how to proceed, Natalie emerged on the upper balcony of the apartment building. With her blond hair floating in the breeze, she took his breath away.

Even from here, he could see the sweet fullness of her mouth and the way a T-shirt clung tantalizingly to her rounded breasts as she descended the exterior stairs. His body reacted with a jolt of arousal.

Natalie was halfway to her car when she stopped to glare at the truck. It looked as if she was saying, "What the heck?"

He got out and strode across the street. "Looks like you've got a problem."

She blinked up at him. "Patrick?"

"I was driving by." That sounded unlikely, didn't it? "I was on my way to being early," he explained, and decided that was even worse. "Never mind why I'm here. Need some help?"

"I'm going to visit Amy Ravenna. I'd like to know what idiots left this here," she said, then answered her own question. "They must be moving into the ground-floor apartment. The tenants moved out last week."

He followed her to the unit. The door stood open, a few items of furniture visible inside. A preteen girl and a little boy sat watching cartoons on a television placed on the floor.

"Hi! I'm Natalie," she said. "We need for somebody to move the truck. Where are your parents?"

"They went to get lunch," the girl said.

"And left you alone?" Patrick asked.

"I'm twelve." She kept her gaze fixed on the screen.

"When will they be back?" Natalie asked.

"I don't know."

The two of them retreated. "Are you in a hurry to meet Amy?" he asked.

"She said I could drop by any time in the next hour or so," she said. "But I hate waiting. I'm also afraid I'm going to chew out those blockheads when they get back. That's not a good way to meet my neighbors."

"I'd be happy to give you a ride." There was nothing wrong with enjoying her company as long as they kept it light.

Natalie considered his offer. "Amy did say she'd like to go shopping later. I guess she could drop me back here."

"Done." Taking her elbow, Patrick guided her toward his car.

"Why did you say you were here?" she asked as she slid into her seat.

"Passing through," Patrick mumbled, and closed the door as soon as she was tucked inside.

When he climbed behind the wheel, he felt Natalie's presence surround him like an embrace. "It smells nice in here," she said. "Do I detect a hint of flowers?"

Patrick started the engine. "I took some to Mrs. McLanahan while she's laid low."

"Her arthritis is really painful," Natalie said. "I dropped by last night with Chinese food. She says it's okay to cheat on her low-cholesterol diet once in a while."

"That was kind of you." He hadn't realized it was a flareup of arthritis that had sidelined the usually vivacious widow. "You're always doing things for people. I know they appreciate it."

"My sister Alana says I help too much." She snuggled against the soft leather upholstery. "She calls me an enabler, but that's not true."

"Helping people doesn't mean you're underwriting their bad habits." Patrick stopped the car at Serene Boulevard. "Which way?"

"Amy lives down in West Serene, near the Black Cat Café." The club was known for its large deli sandwiches and funky music. "Is that too far out of your way?" She knew, of course, about the luncheon.

"Not by much." Patrick didn't mind a little inconvenience. He had plenty of time.

From the corner of his eye, he caught Nat studying him. She pressed her lips together, then touched them with the tip of her tongue as if she had something to say but wasn't sure whether she wanted to say it.

"You feeling okay?" he asked.

"Why, do I look different?" Natalie said.

"Your cheeks are kind of flushed," he said. "You aren't ill, are you?"

"I feel great."

"Good." That conversation had gone nowhere, he thought, and wished he knew what else to say. In silence, they headed south on Serene Boulevard, passing the intersection with Bordeaux Way that led to the main entrance of Doctors Circle.

"How do you feel about kids?" Natalie asked out of the blue.

The question stopped him cold. "That's funny," Patrick said. "My sister made the same point earlier."

"What point?" It was her turn to look confused.

"She believes I was happier when I was in pediatrics. Although I don't understand how you'd know that, since we weren't working together then," he said. "I do miss the children. But in the long run I'm helping more of them in my current position."

"I meant..." She let the sentence trail off. "Look, there's a crafts fair at Outlook Park." Ahead on the right, Patrick saw a cheerful cluster of booths amid the greenery. "Can we stop for a minute? I need to get a couple of presents."

"Fine with me." He rarely browsed through crafts sales, but with Natalie, it ought to be fun.

They parked in the lot and joined the shoppers. Quickly Natalie selected a set of enamel earrings for one friend and a fanciful hat for a niece.

"I've got lots of nieces and nephews," she explained as she chose a couple of extra items for future occasions. "Oh, this one's for me!" She picked up a stuffed bunny.

"You're loyal to your rabbit motif, I see." Patrick had given Natalie a bunny paperweight for Secretary's Day, along with lunch and flowers. Thank goodness his sister had reminded him of the event and pointed out the bunny images on Natalie's coffee mug.

"It's too bad I didn't pick a rarer animal," his secretary said, skirting a stroller. "If I collected hedgehogs, I wouldn't buy so many curios. But rabbits appeal to me."

When she stopped at another booth, Patrick volunteered to carry her rapidly filling shopping bag. "I can at least make myself useful."

"Thanks." She handed it over. "You're not bored, are you?"

"I enjoy watching you shop," he said truthfully.

"Are you sure— Oh, what a cute little coin-box wishing well! I'll buy it for Amy."

She looked far more animated here than at work. Younger and more relaxed, too, the way she had that day on the yacht, Patrick noted as Natalie added yet another item to her purchases.

He imagined he could still smell the sea breeze in her hair. With her, that afternoon, he'd forgotten everything except the joy in her eyes and the luminous pleasure of their coupling.

"Natalie!" A woman with a small boy in tow stopped in front of them. "I never got a chance to thank you for last weekend."

"It was fun," Natalie said.

"Baby-sitting a toddler may be fun, but it's also hard work." To Patrick, the woman explained, "My husband was in the hospital. Thanks to Natalie, I was able to stay at his bedside. Are you one of her brothers?"

"A friend," he said. "I hope your husband's better."

"He's fine now." The woman hung on as her little boy tried to pull free. "Natalie does more for people than anyone else in our church."

"I do not!"

"We all know we can count on you," she said. "And we appreciate it."

Abruptly the little boy broke loose, lost his balance and fell. A wail tore through the air.

"What's the matter, Joey?" His mother squatted beside him.

"Knee hurts!" He pointed to red scrape marks.

"Let me see." Patrick knelt, set aside the shopping bag and took out his handkerchief. "Let's wipe that off until your mom has a chance to wash it."

"Please don't get your handkerchief all—" The woman stopped, because it was too late.

Carefully Patrick cleared away the clinging bits of grass and pebble. "You're very brave," he said.

"Big owie," Joey replied earnestly.

"This is a major owie in anybody's book," Patrick agreed. "You know what? You're going to have a nice scab. Have you ever had a scab before?"

Joey started to nod, then shook his head. He watched the doctor in fascination.

"Don't pick at the scab," Patrick said. "Even if it itches. Any time you start to scratch it, clap your hands together, instead. Can you do that?"

"Yes."

"Show me."

Joey clapped his hands.

Still in a kneeling position, Patrick took a bow. "Thank you."

Joey laughed. His mother scooped him up. "You're wonderful with him. I figured he'd be screaming his head off for the next hour. Can I wash that handkerchief for you?"

"No, thanks." He stuck it in his pocket. "Just make sure you wash and disinfect the scrape."

"You bet!"

After the woman was out of earshot, Natalie said, "You were great with Joey. I'm impressed."

"I'd forgotten how good that feels, working with a child," Patrick said.

He prided himself on how well he knew his own nature. Yet today both his sister and his secretary had pointed out something that, until this moment, he'd pushed from his mind.

Pediatrics. Maybe he'd get back to it someday. The medical center came first, though.

"That wasn't why I asked..." Natalie hesitated as they sauntered down the last row of booths. "I didn't mean whether you like kids as a doctor. I meant..."

Ahead of them, an older woman at a booth waved vigorously toward them. "Look who's here!" she called.

Pink hair floated around the woman's head, and despite the warmth of the day, she wore a paisley shawl over a long, shapeless dress. Her booth was hung with wind chimes, while the counter overflowed with stuffed dolls.

Behind the booth, in a chaise longue, reclined an equally eccentric-looking man. His salt-and-pepper hair was pulled back in a ponytail, and the cutoff sleeves of his T-shirt revealed an eye-catching series of tattoos.

Beside him, Patrick felt Natalie grow tense. Who were these people? he wondered.

The woman gestured them toward her. Natalie released a sigh. "Dr. Barr," she said as she led him forward, "I'd like you to meet my mother."

Chapter Three

As Natalie made introductions, she hoped her unpredictable mother wouldn't say anything offensive. Angie sometimes peppered her speech with four-letter words, and her attitudes toward everything from money to the law were anything but conventional.

Angie seemed too impressed by Patrick to fire off any wild opinions, though, and so did her longtime boyfriend. Although a former biker and drug abuser, Clovis had a good heart.

Only a surprised blink revealed Patrick's reaction to her odd-looking mother. Otherwise, he was the soul of courtesy. Not that Natalie expected anything less from her diplomatic boss.

"Did you make these yourself?" he asked Angie, examining one of the dolls. "They're delightful."

"She makes everything except the wind chimes," said Clovis. "I make those."

"You're both very talented," Patrick said. "I especially like the dolls' expressions." They *were* appealing, Natalie reflected. "I'd like to buy one for my sister."

"You think it's her style?" Natalie had seen the ultramodern home Bernie and her ad-exec husband owned. She couldn't picture the rustic doll fitting in.

"She collects handmade dolls," Patrick explained. "She calls it her secret passion. I usually have a hard time picking out gifts, so I'd better buy one now."

The sight of the doll in his grip reminded Natalie of the baby inside her, and she felt a rush of longing to see him hold their child with this same tenderness. Maybe it would happen. And maybe cows would fly.

"I like your boss," Angie announced. "You should bring him over for dinner sometime."

"Sure. He'd be welcome." Clovis rolled himself a cigarette, using tobacco from a pouch.

Angie's makeshift cooking was the subject of good-humored family jokes, especially about the Thanksgiving when she'd served her guests frozen turkey dinners with made-from-a-mix macaroni and cheese on the side. Patrick would be a good sport, Natalie thought, but she wasn't sure she wanted him to know her relatives quite that intimately.

"I'll get back to you on that, Mom," she said.

Patrick took a couple of dolls into the direct sunlight to make his choice. Other shoppers drifted past, and then a well-dressed man stopped to eye Clovis disapprovingly.

From his high forehead to his sour expression, he was almost a dead ringer for Dr. Sorrell. A few more wrinkles and a small scar on his cheek distinguished Police Chief Finn Sorrell.

"What's in that cigarette?" he demanded.

"Tobacky," Clovis drawled. "Want a drag, Chief?" He held out the partly smoked stick.

"I've got half a mind to take that in for evaluation,"

the chief said. "I guess you wouldn't be stupid enough to smoke something illegal in public, though."

"If you're not interested in shopping, maybe you should go make yourself useful somewhere else, Chief." Angie had never been known to hold her tongue, even around agents of the law. And unfortunately her family had had its share of brushes with Chief Sorrell's department.

While none of the family had committed any major illegal acts, there'd been several run-ins, including domestic quarrels that got out of hand. The police chief obviously hadn't forgotten.

He regarded Natalie with a curled lip. "Helping your mom earn a living?" he asked. "I didn't figure you'd last long at that hospital job."

She couldn't believe his nerve. "I've been working there nearly six years," she said. "I've had two promotions in title and none-of-your-business how many raises."

Angie bristled. "You've got no call to insult my daughter."

"That wasn't an insult, merely an observation." Abruptly the smug expression vanished from Finn's face. "Oh, hello, Patrick. I didn't see you there."

"How are you, Finn?" The doctor, who apparently hadn't heard the conversation, returned one of the dolls and took out his wallet. In his expensive suit and tie, he made a decided contrast to the couple behind the booth.

"What brings you here?" the chief asked.

"My sister's going to love this doll," Patrick said by way of an answer. "Angie, we ought to start carrying your work at the gift shop. Could you put the Doctors Circle logo on the dolls' clothing?"

"Sure thing." Angie enclosed the doll in a sheet of recycled Christmas wrapping paper. "I'll bring some over when they're ready." She handed him a business card. "You can give that to the head of the gift shop, if you don't mind."

"I'll do that. I'm sure she'll love them."

Natalie prayed that the chief wouldn't say anything to Patrick about her past. She didn't know whether her boss had ever gone back and read her job application, but if he had, he knew that when asked whether she'd ever been arrested, she'd answered no.

The truth was, she'd spent one night in Juvenile Hall after being swept up along with some misbehaving friends. Also, during her divorce, a drunken, angry Ralph had once claimed she'd stolen his car. The police had booked her before discovering it was merely a family dispute.

The incidents seemed so minor she didn't figure they counted. After all, she'd been innocent both times. Too bad her arrest record wasn't the only item Natalie had lied about on the form.

To her relief, Finn Sorrell departed with no further unpleasant remarks. It was unfortunate that he had such a bad attitude toward her family, since the police department generally did a fine job in Serene Beach.

"I'm afraid we have to be leaving," Patrick said. "I'm due at the yacht club in twenty minutes."

"Oh!" Natalie didn't want to make him late for the luncheon. "We'd better hurry."

After exchanging farewells with her mother and Clovis, the two of them headed for his car. It was too late to mention her pregnancy now even if she'd wanted to. She could hardly drop such a bombshell and then send Patrick on his way.

Besides, the encounter with Chief Sorrell had stirred Natalie's insecurities. She hoped Amy, with her counseling expertise, could help her figure out what to do.

"YOU CAN'T TELL anybody I'm pregnant," said Natalie, who'd burst out with her story the moment she arrived and found Amy by the pool. Fortunately the other condominium dwellers must have preferred the beach today, leaving the two women with the place to themselves.

"Of course not! I'd never betray a confidence." Her friend began to dry herself with rough thoroughness. She'd completed a brisk swim just as Natalie joined her, and had been so fascinated by the story that she'd stood there dripping while she listened. "Who's the father? Anybody I know?"

Although she'd intended to spill everything, Natalie found that she couldn't. For one thing, telling Amy might put her in a difficult position, since Patrick was indirectly her boss, too. For another, it was simply too private a matter to share. "I'd rather not say. Sorry."

"That's okay." Amy sat on a chaise longue and began toweling her hair. Long-legged and dark-haired, she moved with a coltish lack of vanity. When her hair was semidry, she perched on the chair cross-legged, her elbows resting on her knees.

"You must think I'm a mess," Natalie said, "sleeping with a guy I can't talk about and ending up pregnant."

"I don't think that at all," Amy answered. "In a way, I'm envious."

"Why on earth?"

Her friend shrugged. "It's just that I'm such a tomboy, I've never…I mean, I'm thirty-three years old and I still haven't…''

"Had a baby?" Natalie finished for her. "That's not unusual. You've got lots of time."

"I hope so," her friend said. "Anyway, please go on."

"It's going to be really awkward telling this guy. I'm sure having kids with me is the furthest thing from his mind. Plus, I kind of misled him about my past," Natalie said.

"You're much too sensitive about your family," Amy said. "Nobody else blames you for their weirdness."

"Chief Sorrell does."

"Well, I certainly hope you're not pregnant by him!" They both laughed.

"As I was saying, I don't know what's going to happen when I tell the father." Natalie tilted back her recliner another notch to get comfortable. "We view the world so differently, it's like we grew up on two different planets."

Her friend reflected briefly. Then, "Before yc. tackle the guy, have Heather confirm your pregnancy. Those home kits aren't perfect."

Heather Rourke was an obstetrician on the Doctors Circle staff who sometimes ate lunch with Natalie and Amy. The three of them had similar tastes in movies and books, and twice had gone together to see ice-skating shows.

"She's awfully busy," Natalie said dubiously. "I mean, now that she's taken on more infertility patients, she has a full schedule. Not too busy to see a friend, though, I guess."

"She'll work you in," Amy said. "You know, I hear

Patrick's hiring some big shot to head the new infertility office. I hope Heather gets along with him or her.''

"Heather gets along with everybody," Natalie said. "Okay, I'll give her a call."

Amy finger-combed her long hair, which fell in a tangle around her shoulders. She had a natural beauty of which she seemed unaware. "If she confirms that you're pregnant, you've got to face this boyfriend of yours. Just be prepared. Guys don't always see things the way we do."

"Such as what, for instance?" Natalie said. "I mean, how many ways are there to view a pregnancy?"

"He might bring up adoption," Amy said. "To a guy, that can sound like an attractive way out."

"Adoption?" At this stage of her life, Natalie couldn't imagine going through a pregnancy and then relinquishing the baby. "No way!"

"Don't overreact if he suggests it," Amy said. "Men can be clueless. But keep a good thought. Maybe he loves you."

Natalie sighed. "It's not that simple. This man comes from society. You know what my upbringing was like. I'm in over my head."

"Natalie, you've got class. Everybody knows it."

"Everybody except Dr. Sorrell and his brother," she said. "And maybe I don't have as much class as you think."

"In my book, you do," her friend said loyally.

Speaking of Chief Sorrell reminded Natalie about the crafts bazaar. She dug into her shopping bag. "By the way, I brought you something."

"Nat!" Amy leaned forward. "You're too generous."

"It's fun to do nice things for my pals." Natalie handed her the ceramic wishing well. "Drop in a coin and your wish will come true."

"I wouldn't dare wish for what I want," Amy said.

"Why not?"

"I'm scared of getting in over my head, too," she said. "No, don't ask questions. I'm not going to say another word about it."

Natalie didn't pry. Over the years she'd discovered that, like her, Amy and Heather preferred to keep parts of their lives private. This sort of reserve was one of the things the three women had in common.

As it turned out, Heather's first available appointment wasn't until Wednesday, so Natalie vowed to follow Amy's advice and do nothing until then. Keeping such a volatile secret proved more uncomfortable than she had imagined, though.

Working in a facility full of doctors and nurses, she felt as if everyone could read her condition on her face. Surely they noticed the telltale early signs of pregnancy like flushed cheeks and frequent trips to the bathroom.

Natalie saw Doctors Circle differently now. The bubbling fountain in the courtyard, despite its cherubic sculpture, made her feel queasy. On the other hand, the two front wings and the Birthing Center with its white stucco walls gave her a sense of being surrounded by warmth.

When her duties took her into the Birthing Center, Natalie dawdled as she passed the labor-and-delivery area with its busy triage center. Eight months from now, she might be a patient here. The possibility seemed unreal and miraculous and scary.

"Natalie?" Patrick asked. They were standing by

the antepartum area where pregnant women came for ultrasounds, amniocentesis and monitoring. "Let's eat at the hospital cafeteria, if you don't mind." He made a point of checking out the food quality from time to time, to make sure it maintained high standards.

"You bet." Since she had one more day to wait before her appointment with Heather, Natalie's nerves had nearly vanquished her appetite. But not entirely.

She tucked the color-scheme portfolio under her arm. During the next few months the whole complex was to receive a facelift to coordinate with the remodeled infertility center. She'd been trailing Patrick through the buildings as they visualized how the designer's plans might look.

Gorgeous, that was how. Natalie loved the choices of turquoise, mint-green and sunny yellow, played out in a variety of window treatments and wall coverings.

The cafeteria would benefit from a touchup, that was for sure, she reflected as the two of them got in line. The large room had a lovely vista of a plant-shaded patio, with an outdoor, as well as indoor, eating area, but the nondescript paint had become discolored and the linoleum was worn.

Patrick chose a table in the middle of the crowded room, one of the least-attractive places to sit. Typically, he was too busy assessing the quality of the food to pay attention to his surroundings.

"We need to update the salads," he said. "I'm hardly a food critic, but I find this boring. What do you think?"

Natalie glanced at her bowl of iceberg lettuce, shredded cabbage and a single cherry tomato. "How about some sun-dried tomatoes and feta cheese?"

And a declaration of undying love on your part, she

added mentally. *Or at least a hint that you'd like to get me alone on your yacht again, so that before I risk telling you everything, I know that our interlude meant something to you.*

"Good idea, although the cheese should be served on the side, since not everyone can eat it. Also, the Italian dressing ought to be made with olive oil, instead of soybean oil. It's better for your heart." Patrick made a note on his Palm organizer.

How could the man sit opposite her and remain so blind to her state of mind? Natalie wondered. But then, after working for him for five years, she knew how single-minded Patrick was. Time for a little gentle prompting.

"Now that we've resolved the salad situation, what do you say we move on to other topics?" she murmured.

"Absolutely," he said. "Take the eggplant parmesan. It's not bad at all."

She wanted to give him a poke. "Aside from the food," she persisted, "is there anything you'd like to discuss?"

"As a matter of fact, there is." Looking up, he met her gaze. "Something personal."

Her heart rate sped up. Finally he'd taken notice of her. "Yes?"

Patrick smiled. "I just want to say I'm glad we're back to normal."

"Normal?"

"My behavior on the yacht was inappropriate," he explained. "I don't blame you for being standoffish afterward. I'm glad we're back to our old selves."

Was that what he wanted, to go on forever as boss

and secretary? Sadly Natalie reflected that that was no longer an option.

Sooner or later the truth would become all too apparent. She just hoped it was a whole lot later.

"I'm sure we'll catch some flak from the cafeteria manager about changing the seating around," Patrick continued, failing to notice her silence. "But I like the designer's idea of creating privacy zones. This place feels too much like a high-school cafeteria."

"Right." At the moment Natalie wouldn't care if the designer made people eat on the floor, but she had no intention of saying so.

"Everyone's going to have to be flexible, with all the changes we're planning. They can't fight their own petty turf wars. It'll be worth it." Patrick went on discussing the upcoming modifications.

Gradually, as she listened, Natalie forgot her irritation. She loved hearing the excitement in Patrick's voice and seeing the fire in his brown eyes. When he leaned forward to make a point, his intensity was like a caress, sending thrills down her spine.

She ached to touch his face and bring his mouth to hers. Would it ever happen again?

After they finished eating, they left the Birthing Center and cut across the courtyard. From nearby came the lilting sound of a chorus singing a hymn. The Serenity Fellowship Church, located next door to the medical center, was known for its choir, which practiced several afternoons a week.

The central courtyard, with its fountain and brand-name coffee kiosk adjacent to a breezeway, attracted a cheerful assortment of brown-bagging staffers and family members waiting for patients. Across a small round table, two women were talking earnestly. At another, an elderly couple beamed as their grandchild read from a picture book.

A wistful look flashed across Patrick's face. Following his gaze, Natalie saw two women carrying infants into the Well-Baby Clinic on the first floor of the West Wing. Her spirits lifted. Maybe he was eager to have a child, in which case he might not be so upset when she told him....

"Spencer Sorrell doesn't know how good he has it." Patrick kept his voice low so no one else could hear. "He wants to be a full-time administrator and resents having to examine babies. That's the best part of his job, if only he realized it."

"Do you want to be a pediatrician again?" Natalie asked.

He shook his head abruptly. "Of course not, when I can be accomplishing so much in administration. You've seen the statistics, how birth defects and infant mortality in Serene Beach have dropped each year since this center was established. What more could I ask?"

"If you like babies so much, I'm surprised you haven't had any of your own." As soon as the words slipped out, she wanted to call them back. "I'm sorry. That's none of my business."

"You know what I'm like," Patrick said. "If I had my way, I'd move into my office full-time."

"You seemed to enjoy talking to that little boy at the crafts fair," Natalie said. "Maybe if you spent more time around kids..."

She stopped when they turned right into the East Wing and came within earshot of other people. The workmen sat eating their sack lunches amid piles of sawdust and lumber, so there was no racket from the high-power saws.

On the other side of the foyer, clients were arriving and departing at the radiology department, which provided outpatient mammograms, ultrasounds and X rays. There were also visitors to the laboratory, which lay between radiology and the work zone, and which usually caught the brunt of the noise. After the reconstruction began, some wag had dubbed the area No Man's Lab.

As Natalie and Patrick stepped out of the elevator on the second floor, she saw through the doorway that someone was waiting beside her desk. As they approached, the visitor stood up.

A tall woman with ash-blond hair and blue eyes much like Natalie's, she wore a too-short skirt and a top that failed to cover her navel. It was Candy, her oldest sister.

She rarely popped into Natalie's life except to ask for a favor. Heaven knew what kind of fix she'd gotten herself into this time.

If only Patrick would bowl right into his office without noticing her! She wasn't that lucky, however.

Hurrying toward them, Candy grabbed Natalie's arm. "Sis, I've got to talk to you." She stared at Patrick. "Who's this? Are you a doctor?"

"Yes, I am," he said.

"What kind?"

He blinked, a bit taken aback by her brashness. "A pediatrician."

"Too bad," she said. "Nat, I've absolutely got to have liposuction."

"We can talk about this some other time." Natalie squirmed. "Candy, I'm working."

"I know that!" Her sister tightened her grip on Natalie's arm. "I've got a shot at a swimsuit-modeling job next month. Have you tried on one of those new suits? Never mind, you're only twenty-nine. Wait'll you're…thirty." She'd just knocked three years off her age. "Now here's what I want you to do."

Patrick stood listening, making no move to go into his office. Judging by his expression, he was either shocked or fascinated by this strange creature.

Until now, Natalie had managed to avoid exposing him to her overbearing sister. Her luck had finally run out. She could only stand there and hope the racket downstairs would resume and be loud enough to drown Candy out.

ALTHOUGH HE'D WORKED with Nat for five years, Patrick hadn't met any of her family until this past weekend. They were proving to be an interesting bunch.

"My insurance won't cover liposuction and I can't afford it on a night clerk's salary," Candy continued. "But you work at a medical center! You can find out how to fudge the paperwork so I can make the liposuction look like another kind of operation, something that's covered."

"That's fraud," Natalie said.

"Everybody does it," scoffed her sister.

"Besides, the doctors at our clinics don't perform liposuctions," she said.

"Well, not Dr. Pedes here, obviously." The woman pronounced it Peeds, as in Pediatrics. Patrick had to subdue a chuckle at being so casually dismissed, when most people treated physicians with excessive deference. "Maybe one of the doctors can perform some minor surgery on me and suck out the fat while he's at it.''

"It doesn't work that way," Natalie said. "Candy, I'm not going to help you cheat your insurance company, and no ethical doctor would perform unnecessary surgery."

"It *is* necessary! If I can't get myself in shape in a hurry, I'm out of a career," Candy protested, flinging back her long hair.

"How much does this operation cost?" Natalie asked.

"A couple of thousand dollars."

"I'll lend it to you," she said. "But you're paying me back in installments, starting next month."

"All right." Her sister made a face. "Although I think you're being a chump. All you have to do is help and we could arrange this for free."

"No."

"It's your money," Candy said.

"On loan!"

"Yeah, yeah. I'll let you know the exact amount when I get the surgery scheduled. Nice to meet you, Doc.''

"Nice meeting you, too," Patrick said. Remembering how much work he had to do, he escaped to his office.

Before he closed the door, he heard Natalie's sister say, "Hey, is that guy your boss?"

"Yes."

"He's got a great bod," was the response.

Patrick thought he heard his secretary groan. He was more grateful than ever that his own ultra-dependable sister made his life easier, not more complicated.

Chapter Four

The second floor of the West Wing lay directly across the courtyard from the administration offices. From Heather Rourke's waiting room, Natalie could see the outside of her own window.

It looked a million miles away.

She tried to read the novel she'd brought to pass the time while waiting for her appointment. It was no use. After skimming the same page three times without absorbing the contents, she gave up.

Her cheeks still burned as she remembered yesterday's encounter with Candy. Her sister had been rude to Patrick and she'd proposed to cheat her insurance company.

Patrick hadn't said anything critical, then or later, and Natalie knew he didn't hold her responsible for her sister's lack of ethics. But she hated to think that, when he learned about her deception, he might consider her and Candy to be two of a kind.

When she applied for the job, she'd known that her computer, typing, filing and front-office skills were all first rate. She'd taken secretarial classes and gained experience working for a temp agency.

The woman who handed her the application, however, had startled her by saying, "Dr. Grier insists on a certificate from a secretarial school. You do have one, don't you?"

Instinctively Natalie had nodded. On the application, under "education," she'd listed a certificate that, in fact, she hadn't finished earning.

It had been a long time ago, and Patrick ought to understand. But he'd fired a lab technician for a similar offense.

"Nat? Is that you?" She looked up, startled, to see an old friend, Rita Lopez Beltran. "It's been a long time!"

Rita's husband, Sam, owned the car dealership where Natalie's ex-husband, Ralph, had worked. The two women, near the same age, had gravitated to each other at company picnics. They still saw each other occasionally, since Rita's sister, Loretta Lopez Arista, was the public-relations director for Doctors Circle.

"You look wonderful." Natalie meant it wholeheartedly. Rita was glowing.

"I just found out I'm pregnant, and it's thanks to Dr. Rourke!" gushed the dark-haired woman. "I've been wanting a baby for so long I'm floating on air."

"Congratulations!"

"Please don't tell my sister," Rita added. "Loretta's been trying to get pregnant even longer than I have, and I don't want to upset her."

"She'll find out sooner or later," Natalie pointed out.

"Maybe by then she'll be pregnant herself," Rita said.

"I hope so. I wish the best for you both."

"How are you doing? Any word from Ralph?"

"He's in Texas, working as a mechanic," Natalie

said. "Last month he sent a card and said he was thinking of me. I hope he's not thinking too hard, because I don't want to see him."

"I don't blame you, after the way he behaved. Well, I can't wait to tell my husband the good news. Please remember not to say anything to my sister."

"I promise," Natalie said.

Shortly after Rita left, Heather's nurse, Cynthia Hernandez, called Natalie's name. The young woman proceeded to weigh her and take her temperature. She had a distracted air. There were dark circles under her eyes and a strand of her tied-back dark hair straggled along one cheek.

"Are you feeling okay?" Natalie asked.

"Excuse me?" The young woman looked startled.

"You're a million miles away." Always before, Heather's nurse had struck Natalie as cheerful and outgoing.

"I'm a little tired," Cynthia said. "My boyfriend and I were out late last night. It doesn't interfere with my work, honestly."

"I never suggested it did," Natalie reassured her. "It was a friendly question." Even though she worked for the center's administrator, that didn't mean she pried into everyone's business.

She simply cared about all the people here, staff and patients, who these days were referred to as clients. She cared about Rita and Loretta, and about Cynthia, too.

The nurse asked for a urine specimen, then prepared Natalie for the exam. A few minutes later Heather came bustling into the room, wearing a traditional white coat and stethoscope.

"Nat! So tell me what's going on. Are you feeling ill?" Concern shone in the obstetrician's face. Despite her thirty-six years, Heather looked almost too young to be a doctor, and her intensity and halo of red hair made her seem larger than life.

There was no point in being coy, Natalie told herself. "I think I'm pregnant."

"Let's find out." Within minutes, Heather had examined Natalie, determined the date of her last period and tested the specimen. "You're right. I'd put your due date at around May first."

After Natalie got dressed, they sat down to talk. Patients often commented on how carefully Heather listened to them, and the reason was obvious.

"I don't know how to tell the father," Natalie said. "It's a delicate situation."

"He's not married, is he?" Heather asked.

"No, of course not."

"Good. Someone I know is seeing a married man and I wish I could discourage her," she said.

An image of the nurse flashed into Natalie's mind. Was that why Cynthia had been out late on a Monday night, because her married boyfriend was sneaking around at odd hours? If so, she hoped the young woman came to her senses before she ended up with a dilemma like Natalie's.

"My situation is a little different," she said. "The father might marry me out of a sense of obligation, but...well, there are problems."

Heather gazed at her sympathetically. "It's hard to raise a child alone, although lots of women do it well. Personally, I think it's best if there's a strong father figure."

"Amy mentioned adoption," Natalie said reluctantly. "I don't see how I could give up my baby, though. What if he or she came back years later and reproached me?''

''What if he or she came back years later and thanked you?'' Heather toyed with the edge of her white coat in an uncharacteristically nervous way. ''Never mind. Just because a decision is right for one person doesn't mean it's right for another.''

Natalie got the impression that her friend was talking about an incident from her own life. But if she was, she chose to keep it to herself.

''In any case, the father needs to be told, doesn't he?'' Natalie said. ''I'm assuming I can rely on your nurse's discretion not to feed the gossip mill.''

''Cynthia is utterly trustworthy on that score.'' Heather stopped fiddling with her coat. ''The best decision is the one that makes you happy. Sooner or later, your condition is going to become obvious, but in the meantime, there's no rush. Take your time figuring out what you want to do.''

The idea was comforting, to focus on the moment and let the future take care of itself. Natalie knew instantly that this was the advice she'd been seeking.

''You're right. I'm going to wait,'' she said. ''He'll discover the truth eventually. No need for me to throw it in his face.''

''Don't wait too long,'' Heather warned.

''Define 'too long.'''

''Nine months.'' They both smiled.

Natalie stood up. ''I know you've got other patients to see. I'm sorry to take up so much of your time.''

''Not at all! I'm glad to help,'' Heather said. ''Don't forget to make an appointment for your next checkup. Cynthia will give you information and a prescription for vitamins. Ask her to see if we have any free samples for you.''

"Thanks," Natalie said. "You've helped more than you know."

PATRICK WAS BEGINNING to wonder if he'd made a mistake by installing videoconferencing technology on his computer. Even without it, he'd have had to deal with Jason Carmichael by telephone, but at least he wouldn't have had to face the other doctor's irritated glare.

"No one mentioned that the new facility wouldn't be ready until April," Jason growled. "I've given notice and put my house on the market so I could arrive in February, as we discussed. Now suddenly there's a delay!"

"No, there isn't."

"I think I know a delay when I see one!" the man snapped.

Patrick reminded himself that Jason was one of the nation's leading infertility specialists, and it was a coup to have lured him from Virginia to serve as chief of the new infertility office. So what if the man was known to be abrasive? He got results with patients, and that was what counted.

"I thought you understood that I want you to get established before the opening," Patrick said. "I've arranged to set aside a temporary office for you in our West Wing. I'm sure you'll find it more than adequate."

"I'll have to move my office? That's inconvenient, but it's too late to change things now, I suppose," the man grumbled. With his dramatic black hair and green eyes, he might be considered handsome, but his high-handed attitude made it hard to see him as anything but a potential pain in the neck.

"Sorry about the misunderstanding." Patrick was determined to remain diplomatic. He'd provided Jason with full information when they met in person last June during a medical convention, but apparently the man hadn't been paying attention.

"The main reason I called is that I have to fly to Los Angeles next week to speak at a seminar," Jason said. "If you want to hold a press conference to announce that you're hiring me, it's the only time I'll be available until after the holidays."

"Next week?" Patrick had planned to schedule the press conference for early November, after the Oktoberfest fund-raiser at his estate. "That's short notice."

"Flying to the West Coast again would take too much time from my schedule," Jason said. "I can pop down to Serene Beach on Tuesday afternoon or Wednesday morning, take your pick." He made his offer sound like a great concession.

There was no point in arguing. Patrick was counting on the news of hiring Dr. Carmichael to generate excitement and bring in more donations for the Endowment Fund. "Tuesday afternoon," he said.

The physician nodded. "Fine. Let my secretary know if you need her to fax you more information about me. By the way, since my current secretary can't relocate, it's essential that you hire someone to be on staff no later than January."

"Before you arrive?"

"I want my files set up and my appointments in order when I get there. Someone experienced and reliable."

"Anything else?" Patrick asked, trying to keep the edge from his voice.

"That's all I can think of. Call my secretary with the time when you get the press conference set up."

"I'll do that." Patrick gritted his teeth to keep from adding a sarcastic "sir," along with a salute.

Jason clicked off. Patrick stared blurrily at the computer screen. *He's a brilliant doctor. Keep that in mind.* Putting up with rudeness was a small sacrifice compared to the prestige of landing a nationally known specialist like Dr. Carmichael.

Patrick buzzed Natalie, and she appeared in the doorway, her blue eyes inquisitive. Her vulnerable air and the silkiness of her summer dress did alarming things to Patrick's masculine instincts.

He dragged his mind back to the subject at hand. "I need to meet with Loretta Arista. Jason Carmichael's going to be in town next week and it's our only chance to schedule a press conference."

Natalie made a note on her pad. "Next week? That's sudden."

"Dr. Carmichael likes to have things his own way," Patrick said, then added, "Once he settles in, I'm sure he'll be fine. By the way, the videoconferencing works quite well."

"I'll have to try it sometime. Maybe with my sister Alana in Oregon." Natalie walked over to stand behind him, regarding the videocamera fixed atop the computer. Patrick tapped a button and suddenly an image appeared on the screen, live and in motion: her standing, him seated, both looking out at themselves.

"Does that make you feel like a shoplifter under surveillance?" he joked, and saw his image move as he spoke.

"It makes me feel like a movie star." She took a closer look. "Well, maybe an actress in a low-budget production."

As she brushed against him, Patrick caught the scent of almonds and honey. Bath soap, he thought, and visualized her running a bar of soap along her bare skin as she stood sleek and naked in the shower, hair tousled around her shoulders. He could almost taste the almonds.

On the screen Patrick saw his eyes dilate and his lips part as if he was about to sample something wonderful. Startled, he clicked off the camera.

Natalie took an abrupt step back, as if she, too, had snapped out of a daydream. "I'll call Loretta," she said, and headed for the door.

"One more thing." She halted. "Our new specialist wants a top-notch secretary. I'm relying on you to find her for him."

"Me?" Natalie asked. "Why not Human Resources?"

"Because we need someone out of the ordinary," Patrick said. "Human Resources can place the ads and do the initial screening, but I want you to interview the candidates. She'll have to be a self-starter, reliable and experienced. Someone like you."

"The hard part is going to be saying no to applicants," Natalie admitted. "I hate disappointing people."

"You'll hate it even more if you disappoint Jason Carmichael," Patrick said. "By the way, one more qualification—his secretary needs a thick skin."

"I'll call the zoo and see if they have any alligators who can type," she said.

After Natalie left, Patrick stared after her for a bemused moment. He didn't know how he would function in this crazy-making job if it wasn't for her. His predecessor, Dr. Grier, had been so high-handed that he'd destroyed staff morale and sent donations plummeting, but at least he'd had the sense to hire Natalie.

Thinking about her reminded Patrick of her mother's dolls. With a smile, he picked up the phone and called Miriam James, the gift-shop manager, to give her Angie's number.

By the time he hung up, the public-relations director was waiting to see him.

"WE'LL HAVE TO HUSTLE to get the press kits ready in time, but otherwise, there shouldn't be a problem." Sitting on the far side of Patrick's desk, Loretta Arista gave a knowing nod to Natalie. "I could use all the help I can get, of course."

"Count on me," Natalie said. Remembering Rita's confidential disclosure about her sister trying to get pregnant, she wished she had a magic wand so she could help. Well, maybe the great Dr. Jason Carmichael was the answer to Loretta's prayers.

"If you hit any roadblocks, I'll run interference," Patrick said. "If you like, we can hold the press conference at the yacht-club ballroom."

"I'd prefer our own auditorium." Slim and businesslike, Loretta wore her dark hair short, with a white streak in the front that gave her a sophisticated air. "That will make it easier for our key staff members to attend, even if it is a less-than-elegant location." The auditorium was located in the basement of the Birthing Center. "We can host a reception afterward in the conference room next to it."

Not only top staff members but patrons would be

invited. The hiring of a new infertility director affected them all.

"I'm debating whether we should continue to keep his identity a secret," Patrick said. "It won't be easy, with us running off press releases and making copies of his photograph to hand out when he arrives."

"It's more exciting if it's a surprise, to the press, as well as to everyone else," Loretta said. "Let's try to keep it under wraps."

As Natalie took notes, Patrick and Loretta went over the details of the presentation and the reception. As always, she was impressed by the way her boss focused on details without losing sight of the big picture.

She tried not to stare at him. Patrick always seemed too muscular and vibrant to fit behind a desk. She knew exactly where he *did* fit, and how it felt. In bed, out of bed…

A few minutes ago, standing behind him, she'd had an outrageous urge to lean forward until her breasts pressed into his back. She'd imagined him turning around and pulling her onto his lap, after which their clothes would rapidly disappear. Thank goodness he couldn't read minds.

"This won't interfere with planning for the Oktoberfest, I hope," Patrick said.

That lighthearted evening celebration was less than two weeks away. Political leaders, entertainment and sports figures and corporate heads from across Southern California had been invited.

"Don't worry, I'm on top of both events." Loretta stood up. "Well, I'd better get to work." She exited, with Natalie behind her.

"You're being a good sport about this last-minute press conference," Natalie said in the outer office.

"I'm thrilled to learn that Dr. Carmichael's coming on board," Loretta said. "There've been rumors about a specialist being hired, but I didn't know he would be so prominent."

"A lot of women will want his services, I'm sure."

"I'm going to be first in line," the PR director said frankly. "I'm thirty-four and I have to tell you, I'm getting desperate. Dr. Rourke's tried her best, but I need a heavy hitter with a more high-tech approach."

"He won't be on staff until February," Natalie pointed out.

"With luck, I'll be pregnant by then," Loretta said. "If not, though, I intend to be number one on his appointment calendar."

Natalie smiled. "Good for you."

After the other woman left, Natalie put in a call to Human Resources about hiring an executive secretary, then began typing up her notes for Patrick. When the phone rang, she answered briskly, "Director's office."

"Nattie?" The nasal male voice was pumped with enthusiasm. "Honey, it sure is good to hear your voice!"

No, no, no! "What do you want, Ralph?" It was typical of her ex-husband to call her at the office, where she was less likely to slam down the phone.

"We've got a lot of catching up to do while I'm in town," he said. "Let's have dinner."

"I wouldn't have dinner with you if you flew me to Paris to eat lobster."

"Honey, you know I'd do that if I could," he said with a false, jovial note. "I was thinking more along the lines of Sizzler. That used to be one of your favorite restaurants."

"It still is, as long as you're not in it," Natalie said.

"Ralph, we have nothing to discuss. What are you doing in Serene Beach, anyway?"

"I'm here to mend old fences," he said. "I know I owe you an apology."

"More to the point, you owe me the five thousand dollars I spent clearing up your bills," she said.

"If I did, would you have dinner with me?"

"I'd consider sitting on the other side of McDonald's and throwing French fries at you," she said. "Or better still, hand grenades. Don't tell me you moved back here from Texas."

"I'm just visiting. But I figure…"

"Thank goodness for that." Surely her ex-husband wasn't crazy enough to think he had any chance of winning her back, although he had a talent for spinning tall tales and then believing them. "I hope you're visiting someone other than me."

"Nattie, I know I got on your bad side—"

"Don't try to minimize what you did to me." Lying, drinking, absconding and sticking her with his bills— that ought to be grounds for life imprisonment, if there was any justice. "Ralph, I've got work to do. Please don't contact me again."

"I only want to be forgiven."

"Talk to a minister. I'm not in the forgiveness industry," she said, and hung up.

Natalie buried her face in her hands and waited, hoping the phone wouldn't ring again. It didn't.

It was too much to hope, though, that Ralph would give up that easily.

Chapter Five

"Uncle Pat! I lost my goggles in the deep end!" Eight-year-old Kip dripped water onto the poolside cement as he presented what to him was obviously an emergency.

Trees shaded the noonday sun, their shadows dappling the curved pool on the Barr estate. Although September was a hot month in Southern California, this close to the ocean a breeze kept the temperatures comfortable.

"I'll get them for you." Although he often worked on Saturdays, Patrick had volunteered to baby-sit his two nephews while his sister attended a friend's wedding shower. Her husband, who usually watched them on Saturdays, was tied up with an advertising project on deadline.

Kent, age six, sailed his plastic boat around the shallow end. He frowned in concentration as he balanced a series of rings atop the boat.

It was fascinating to watch the boys grow and change, Patrick reflected as he and Kip paced alongside the pool, looking for the goggles in the water below. The boys' personalities—Kip adventurous and impulsive, Kent serious and precise—had unfolded magically over the years.

From his pediatric work, Patrick knew plenty about child development. Seeing it up close, however, was delightfully unpredictable.

"There!" He spotted the goggles, suspended about halfway down the ten-foot depth. "I'll get the net."

His nephew squinted at him in the sunshine. "Oh, come on, Uncle Pat. Aren't you going to dive for them?"

In the shallow end, Kent paused in his self-appointed task. "Yeah, we haven't seen you dive all summer."

"It isn't summer," Patrick teased. "It's autumn."

"Like we didn't know!" said Kip, who alternated between pride at being a third-grader and annoyance at having to do homework.

"As a matter of fact, I dive in the early mornings as part of my daily exercise," Patrick said. He worked out conscientiously, despite his busy schedule.

"That doesn't count," Kent replied.

"Yeah, if we don't see it, it doesn't count," echoed his older brother.

"If I dive, will you both go and change clothes without giving me an argument?" Patrick asked. "Your mother should be back in half an hour, and I'm supposed to have you ready for soccer practice."

"Two dives," Kent said. "One for each of us."

"One where you twist," Kip said. "And a somersault."

"Yeah," agreed his brother.

"You guys drive a hard bargain," Patrick pretended to complain.

"Go get my goggles!" Kip folded his arms, looking like a miniature of his father. Mike, an advertising executive, could act stern when the occasion called for it, but it was never long before his quick mind darted away, engaged by some fresh idea.

"Okay, but don't forget your part of the bargain." Shrugging off the T-shirt he'd worn over his swim trunks, Patrick stepped onto the board.

As soon as he felt the springy wood beneath his bare feet, he entered a carefully calibrated interplay between his muscles and the responsive board. Buoyantly, he strode forward, gave a powerful thrust downward and launched himself into the air.

Patrick spiraled through space in an instant of free flight. Then his shoulders tightened and he straightened his arms to make a clean entry into the water.

He surfaced in mid-pool. "How was that, guys?"

"A perfect ten!" Kip enthused.

"A big zero," Kent said. "You forgot the goggles."

Patrick pretended to glower. "That's all the thanks I get?"

"A deal's a deal," said his younger nephew.

The somersault proved more difficult than anticipated. Being thirty-eight didn't feel old until Patrick tried to duplicate his youthful athletic prowess, he discovered as he went past vertical on his entry. His shoulders smarted from the impact but at least, on the way back up to the surface, he remembered to collect the goggles.

"That was great!" said Kip when his uncle tossed them to him. "You went all the way around."

"You nearly did a flop," corrected Kent. Trust the little scientist to notice a detail like that.

"It looked pretty darn good to me." Natalie's voice sent prickles up Patrick's spine as he lifted himself from the pool.

Water sluiced down his face. Not until he grabbed a towel and wiped his eyes did he get a good look at her.

She'd left her hair loose, framing her face with bedroom softness. In a polo shirt and shorts, her curvy figure issued a mute invitation.

But not for him, Patrick reminded himself. "Something wrong at the office?" He assumed Natalie had gone in this morning, as he would have done himself if not for his promise to his sister. The absence of interruptions made Saturdays a great time to catch up on paperwork.

"We got a fax I thought you'd want to see before Monday, so you can prepare yourself," she said.

"That sounds ominous." He didn't want to review a fax. He wanted to watch Natalie put on a swimsuit and slip into the water beside him. Better yet, he'd like to be alone with her in this secluded pool, and forget the bathing suits.

Alone? That reminded him, they had company. "Natalie, you remember Kip and Kent."

"Sure thing. Hello, fellas." She smiled at his nephews.

"Hi, Natalie!" Kip waved his goggles at her. "Want to watch me sneak up on my brother underwater and tip over his boat?"

"You better not!" Kent cried.

"What she wants to do is watch you both go into the house and come back out in your soccer uniforms," Patrick said.

"All right." Kent lifted his boat from the water. "We did make a bargain."

"Yeah, but we didn't know Natalie was coming,"

Kip protested. "I want to show her how my goggles work."

"Some other time." Patrick began toweling off.

Natalie's gaze swept his bare chest and furred legs before she averted it. He felt his heart rate quicken. So she wasn't indifferent to him as a man, he noted with mingled pleasure and caution.

"We have to keep our word or Uncle Pat won't trust us next time," Kent said.

Logic rarely worked on Kip. "Just one more dip." Without waiting for permission, he fastened the goggles into place and jumped in the water.

Kent stood hugging his boat. "I'm not going in."

"I knew I could rely on you." Patrick wondered how two children from the same parents could have such different personalities.

Kip paddled around underwater for a minute before emerging. "How was that?"

"Impressive," Natalie said.

Satisfied, he went off with his brother. The two of them disappeared through the trees in the direction of the house.

Patrick pulled on his T-shirt. "What's in the fax?"

She handed him a couple of sheets. The top one was a memo from Quentin Ladd, a neonatologist scheduled to arrive in a few weeks to fill a vacancy on the Well-Baby Clinic staff. It was addressed to Patrick. Under "Subject" Quentin had written, "You've got to be kidding!"

"This guy doesn't stand on formality," Patrick noted dryly. At their interview a few months earlier, the young doctor had struck him as outgoing and witty, and the memo's tone strengthened that impression.

"Read on," Natalie said.

According to the fax, Dr. Ladd had received a list of Rules of Conduct from his new boss, Spencer Sorrell. "That's odd," Patrick said. "The employee handbook discusses professional conduct, but I don't recall any list of rules."

"It's attached." Natalie's mouth quirked as she observed him. "You'll find it entertaining."

Patrick flipped to the next sheet, which was entitled, "Rules of Conduct for Well-Baby Clinic Staff." Spencer had even given himself a byline. The man was becoming insufferable. "He should have run this by me before sending it out."

"He should have run it by his common sense, too." She was grinning.

Patrick went down the list. With his usual pedantry, the chief pediatrician had belabored the obvious: staff members were to arrive on time, be prepared to work occasional holidays and weekends, treat clients politely and so on.

Then, apparently not satisfied with telling people what they already knew, Spencer had added a few touches of his own. "You are not to date or form romantic attachments to fellow staff members," he'd written. "Also, remember that your off-duty conduct reflects on the clinic. Drunkenness, inappropriate clothing and scandalous behavior will not be tolerated."

Patrick groaned. "I see why Dr. Ladd says we've got to be kidding."

"I want to know what Dr. Sorrell considers to be inappropriate clothing in Southern California, where some people wear shorts to church," Natalie said. "Is he going to serve as the one-man fashion police?"

At the end of the fax, Quentin had handwritten: "Is this your official policy? Maybe you should issue us all collars and leashes, but I have to say, I draw the line at eating dog biscuits.''

"Fax him on Monday and say it's a joke," Patrick said. "I'll have a talk with Spencer." He returned the pages to Natalie.

Their hands met. Although the contact lasted only an instant, heat flooded through him, and he saw her eyes widen as if she, too, felt the sudden connection.

With her free hand, Natalie reached out and fingered his damp T-shirt. "Speaking of clothing inappropriate for the office, I happen to like yours."

A deep-seated yearning for her hit Patrick like a tidal wave. He hadn't stopped wanting her for a single moment since that evening on the yacht more than a month ago. He just hadn't realized it until now.

He touched a wisp of her pale hair. "It doesn't matter what you wear, Nat. I still see you the way you were that night. Undressed. Beautiful."

Her breathing quickened. "We shouldn't be talking this way."

"We're both adults. We can do what we like." Patrick stroked her cheek, then down her shoulder and along the edge of one full breast.

It was pointless to resist. He pulled her against him and kissed her.

Natalie tensed briefly and then she yielded, molding herself against him. Fire seared away Patrick's caution and he held her tight.

She was so soft, so utterly feminine. He didn't know how they'd kept apart for this long.

On the far side of the grounds, a car turned into the driveway. Out of sight behind the trees, it purred toward the house. Bernie was back.

"We'll continue this later," Patrick said gruffly, releasing Natalie with regret.

"No, we won't." She moved away, her cheeks flushed, and blinked at the wrinkled fax papers she still held in one hand. "What were we thinking?"

"Maybe we think too much," he heard himself say, and wondered from which unsuspected corner of his psyche this recklessness sprang.

An impish light flashed in her gaze. "I believe we just broke all of Dr. Sorrell's rules of behavior," she said. "I hope we don't bring scandal and ruin on Doctors Circle."

Patrick would have liked to give a clever response, but he wasn't in a joking mood. "We need to have a long talk. To figure out where we stand."

"We don't stand," Natalie answered tartly. "When we're alone, we have this tendency to end up horizontal."

"That's what I don't comprehend," he admitted. "This sort of conduct isn't like me."

"Surprise! You're as human as the rest of us." He couldn't read the expression on her face. Amusement? Frustration?

Maybe Spencer wasn't entirely wrong when he opposed romantic attachment between staff members. The problem was, people's emotions couldn't be clicked on and off like light switches. "I don't see how we can deny…"

"Denial is a normal mental state," Natalie replied. "We should both cultivate it."

"Are you sure?"

"Positive," she said. "Now let's go say hello to your sister." She headed for the house and, reluctantly, he followed.

NATALIE WISHED she had a video of Patrick's sculpted body flipping off that diving board so she could play it over and over when she was alone. No matter. It was etched into her memory with a sensuality no camera could capture.

She wasn't sorry she'd kissed him. Or that he'd kissed her, whichever came first. They knew each other so well, worked so closely, that it was sometimes hard to remember whose impulse had sparked what action.

Natalie kept thinking that he was going to tune in to her pregnancy, as if the truth could transmit itself from her psyche to his while they were kissing. It hadn't happened, though, which left her exactly where she'd been ever since she saw Heather.

Procrastinating. And doing her best to keep both her boss and her emotions under control.

She turned her attention to Bernadette Barr Lincoln, better known as Bernie. When she got out of the car and spotted Natalie, she waved enthusiastically and hurried over.

"I haven't seen you in ages!" Although she was a darling of Serene Beach's wealthy set, Bernie always treated Natalie as if they were close friends and social equals. "You look great." She pursed her lips. "Hmm. A bit voluptuous, if I may say so."

It was too early in the pregnancy for Natalie to have put on much weight, yet she'd become aware of changes in her body. Larger breasts was one of them.

"Exercises," she said. "They build up the pectoral muscles."

"Well, it's none of my business," Bernie said. It was obvious from her tone that she didn't mean it.

"Welcome back, sis." Coming alongside, Patrick placed his hand lightly on Natalie's back. The instinctive gesture startled them both, and they leaped apart with almost comical alarm.

Well, great. If Bernie hadn't suspected their relationship before, she did now.

"Did the boys drive you crazy?" she asked, tactfully refraining from comment.

"They were great," Patrick said.

"I've got to run." Natalie waved the fax, although she had no need to respond to it until Monday. "There's a lot of work to do."

"See you again soon," Bernie said.

In the parking bay, Natalie retrieved her dented hatchback from beside Bernie's Lexus. She drove home slowly, her body humming from Patrick's nearness.

There was something appealing about a strong man who lost control when she came near. Too appealing. And dangerous, because she was in danger of losing control, too.

If Natalie wasn't careful, she'd blurt out the truth about everything. One misstep and all she'd worked for might evaporate: her job and Patrick's respect. Sure, as a decent man, he'd provide child support, but every check would burn with the sting of his rejection.

No, she had to keep their worlds separate until she figured out what she wanted to do. From now on, Natalie vowed, she'd resist him. She would put him right out of her thoughts. Patrick and his slim hips and that well-developed chest, gleaming in the sunlight...

Yeah, she'd forget all about how it felt to hold him. Any century now.

SPENCER AVOIDED Patrick's phone calls all day Monday. It wasn't until shortly before Tuesday's press conference that the man showed up at the administrator's office. The timing was probably intentional, since the meeting would have to be short.

Patrick handed him the faxed list of rules. "We need to talk about this."

The older man's nose twitched. His hulking posture reminded Patrick of a bull. "Where'd you get it?"

"You should have shown it to me before distributing it," Patrick said, avoiding a direct answer out of respect for Dr. Ladd's privacy.

"Is there a problem?" Spencer asked, as if there couldn't possibly be. With his large build and high forehead, the doctor presented an imposing appearance that might have intimidated a less confident man than Patrick.

"Yes," Patrick replied quietly but firmly. "There's such a thing as a chain of command."

There was a brief, disgruntled silence before the response came. "Dr. Grier never interfered with the way I run my department. In fact, he expected me to be his successor." The man's nostrils flared. Now he resembled not merely a bull but an angry one.

Patrick had been keenly aware, when he sought the director's position, that the other man considered himself a shoe-in. However, the medical center had been at a critical point, unable to afford a misstep, and the board of directors had evaluated all the candidates thoroughly.

The applicants had included several outsiders, along with Spencer and Patrick, who'd resigned his own seat on the board in order to apply. His sister had replaced him but abstained from voting, so it was Noreen McLanahan and the three other members who'd made the selection based in part on the recommendation of the search committee. Nevertheless, Spencer seemed convinced that Patrick had won out of pure favoritism.

"All rules must be approved by me and reviewed by our counsel for legal reasons," Patrick said. "You could provoke a lawsuit for interfering with our employees' rights."

"It had to be Quentin Ladd who sent you that," Spencer said. "That's his smart-aleck comment written at the end, isn't it? I'm sorry I went along with your recommendation to hire him."

"Stick to the point." Patrick had learned that it was in the pediatrician's nature to stir up trouble and that attempts to placate him only brought more demands, so he didn't bother to try. "In future, you are not to issue any rules, press releases or public statements in the name of Doctors Circle unless I say so. Is that clear?"

Spencer's mouth opened as if to argue. Something in Patrick's expression must have convinced him it would be fruitless, however. He shrugged and got to his feet. "Have it your way." He left without saying goodbye.

Patrick glanced at his watch. Loretta and Natalie had gone to set up the auditorium for the press conference and prepare for the reception afterward. With about twenty minutes to go, the press was probably already filing in, along with staff members and patrons.

Jason should have arrived half an hour ago. Perhaps he was waiting in the outer office with no one to announce him.

Patrick stepped through the door. He saw no sign of Jason, but a dark-haired woman was bent over Natalie's desk, writing a note.

"Can I help you?" he asked.

A young, strained face angled toward him. He recognized her as one of the staff nurses. "Dr. Rourke asked me to drop off some prenatal vitamins for Natalie. I was downstairs at the lab so I just popped up."

"I'm sorry?" Patrick couldn't make sense of her explanation. Why would Natalie be collecting someone else's prenatal vitamins?

"A bunch of samples were delivered this morning, and Dr. Rourke knows we all like to save money," the nurse said. Cynthia Hernandez was her name, he recalled. "We didn't have any when Natalie came in."

"When she came in?" he repeated, feeling as if he'd missed some vital point.

"I'm sorry. I shouldn't be discussing a patient with anyone, even you, Dr. Barr." Cynthia folded her note and wrote Natalie's name on the outside.

"It's all right," he said automatically, while trying to absorb what he'd heard. "She'll be back after the press conference."

"Oh, that's right! I forgot she'd be over there. Dr. Rourke's going, too." The nurse made a weak attempt at a smile. "Forget I said anything."

"You bet," Patrick answered, and watched with a sinking sensation as she departed.

Natalie might have consulted Heather for a routine physical. But there was no reason for the obstetrician to send over prenatal vitamins unless...

...his secretary was pregnant.

Patrick leaned against the desk. It was six weeks since they'd been together. Time enough to confirm a pregnancy. But if he was the father, why hadn't she told him?

He'd used protection, of course. While they were relaxing following the second time, he'd found the condom out of place, but he'd assumed that it had slipped afterward. He was sure—almost sure—that it had been positioned correctly while they were making love.

Still, Natalie was either pregnant or helping out a friend. He needed to talk to her as soon as possible and clear up the matter.

Through the door, he saw the elevator doors open. Out strode a tall man with black hair and angry green eyes.

"Who ever heard of a traffic jam during lunch hour?" snapped Jason Carmichael. "For Pete's sake, it nearly made me late. Well? Where's the press conference?"

"I'll take you there," Patrick said and steered the specialist back to the lift. He would have to wait to talk to Natalie. But not any longer than absolutely necessary.

Chapter Six

"There he is!" Loretta Arista grabbed Natalie's arm in excitement as they peered out of the conference room adjacent to the auditorium. "He's gorgeous! I'll bet my reproductive organs get one glimpse of him and start behaving themselves!"

"You can't get pregnant from the way a man looks," remarked Noreen. Although smartly clad in a designer suit, the gray-haired patron had insisted on making punch and helping set out hors d'ouevres. "If you could, we'd all have babies coming out our ears. Still, he is a stallion, isn't he?"

Natalie could see Noreen's point, but in her opinion, the black-haired doctor marching down the hall wasn't a patch on the man beside him. Patrick might be an inch shorter than Jason Carmichael, but he had a more athletic build. And she knew how firm those muscles were beneath the shirt and suit jacket.

Spotting them, Patrick brought over his guest. He introduced Dr. Carmichael to the three women, who each received a handshake and a stare from the piercing green eyes. The man was definitely going to turn heads among the local females, Natalie thought.

"The press is in position already," Loretta said.

"There's the *L.A. Times,* the *Orange County Register,* two TV stations..."

"I'm surprised they found their way to the basement," Jason said. "Your auditorium is tucked in back of nowhere, wouldn't you say?"

"Consider yourself lucky that Dr. Barr brought you down the rear elevator," Noreen said. "Usually he takes people through surgical admitting and they have to get prepped."

Her remark startled a laugh from the obstetrician. "I'm glad he spared me that." He looked younger and far more pleasant when he smiled, Natalie thought.

Then she noticed Patrick studying her with an unreadable expression, his eyes fixed on her abdomen. No, surely she was imagining that.

Loretta consulted her watch. "Time to start. Let's go on in. Some of these reporters may be on deadline."

She took charge of Jason. Patrick offered his arm to Noreen, who said, "I'm not decrepit yet, young man. Or are you flirting with me?"

"Of course," he said.

"Liar!" She laughed. "I love a handsome rogue, don't you, Natalie?"

"He's a scoundrel, all right," she said dryly, and followed the pair of them to where Loretta and Jason had paused before entering the auditorium. In low tones, the public-relations director was briefing her charge on how she would introduce him to the audience.

From the end of the hallway bustled a late-arriving staffer. Natalie lifted her hand in greeting when she recognized Heather.

Her friend's answering smile froze on her face. She stared at Jason, stunned.

When he noticed Heather, his eyes narrowed. Then he stepped forward to shake hands. "It's nice to see you again, Doctor." His tone was briskly professional.

"Yes, it is," she answered stiffly.

Concern showed on Patrick's face as he gazed from one to the other. "I didn't realize you two were acquainted."

"We've met." Heather didn't elaborate.

Natalie could feel frost forming on the walls. The two must have run into each other at a medical conference, and evidently they hadn't hit it off. She could see Patrick registering that, too.

"It's show time," Loretta said, and led the way into the auditorium. Jason turned away from Heather without another word.

The publicity session went well, in Natalie's opinion. Dr. Carmichael was charming to the press. After they recovered from their surprise, they asked intelligent questions about the procedures he would perform and what difference he might make to infertile couples.

"There are already many highly regarded specialists in Southern California, of course, but we're not in competition because the need is great," he told them. "In my practice, clients can expect the latest in technology along with my own cutting-edge experience. I never want to give anyone false hope, but my percentage of successful pregnancies has been increasing steadily."

Seated nearby on the stage, Loretta beamed at him. In the audience, Heather kept her attention fixed on a spot near the ceiling.

At the conclusion, the patrons and staff applauded loudly. Loretta invited everyone to join them next door for refreshments. Although the TV crews and reporters departed, along with some of the staff, quite a few people crowded into the adjoining chamber.

Natalie scurried about refilling the coffeepot, replenishing the hors d'oeuvres and making sure there were plenty of napkins, paper plates and utensils. At the same time, she couldn't help tuning into the hubbub around her.

Voices buzzed excitedly. Most of the staffers and patrons were openly pleased at this prestigious addition to their community, and Jason accepted their welcome with a pleasant if distant smile.

Several times his gaze strayed to Heather. She kept her attention on the snack table.

As for Patrick, he seemed distracted to Natalie. Once, he started toward her, but was intercepted by other people and drawn into a discussion. He made no attempt to approach her again.

"Let me take over for you." Noreen appeared at Natalie's side. "I enjoy having something to do."

"You've done enough already," she protested. "You should enjoy yourself."

"I didn't get involved with Doctors Circle for a lark," the older woman said. "You know, Natalie, my husband and I were never able to have children, and I couldn't persuade him to adopt. I want to help others, but my motives aren't entirely altruistic. Getting old can be a lonely business unless you keep yourself occupied."

"We love having you around," Natalie said. In addition to making donations and serving on the board of directors, Noreen volunteered three days a week with the Circle Guild. She helped staff the gift shop and delivered flowers to patients.

"And I love being here. Now go talk to people,"

the widow said. "I can see you're buzzing with questions about Dr. Carmichael and a certain lady physician. No need to tell me what you find out—I'm not nosy. But you and Dr. Rourke are friends, and you ought to let her know you care."

"I am a little concerned," Natalie admitted. "Plus, I think Dr. Barr was looking for me. Thanks, Noreen."

"My pleasure."

Natalie scanned the room for her boss. Across the crowd, she saw him answer a call on his cell phone. He listened briefly, then stepped outside to finish the conversation.

Not wanting to disturb him, she searched for Heather and found her lurking in the farthest corner of the room from where Jason held court. "How are you doing?"

"Fine. How about you?" The doctor shook back her mass of red hair and regarded Natalie fondly. "By the way, I sent Cynthia over a while ago with some prenatal vitamins. You should find them on your desk."

"Thanks." In the back of Natalie's mind, a warning light flashed. She hoped the vitamins weren't sitting where Patrick might see them. Still, he was so absorbed with the press conference, the odds were he hadn't paid any attention. "What do you think of our new staff member?"

"He's an excellent physician," Heather said.

"You've met before, I take it."

"At a conference about six months ago," she confirmed without elaborating.

"Was there some kind of disagreement?" Natalie asked. "I couldn't help noticing the two of you didn't exactly leap into each other's arms."

Heather winced. "What an image!"

"Judging by how handsome he is, lots of women would love the idea."

"Lots of women aren't me. Let's just say that he and I don't see eye to eye." The other woman bit into a stuffed mushroom with such ferocity that Natalie guessed she'd rather be taking a chomp of Dr. Carmichael.

Their mutual discomfort might stem from a professional difference of opinion, but Natalie doubted it. Heather's reaction seemed somehow personal. "I hope you'll be able to work together."

"Of course we will," said her friend. "We'll both be busy with our patients." After a moment's hesitation, she added, "Nat, I appreciate your concern, but honestly, there's nothing to worry about."

"Okay." Whatever had taken place between the pair, it was behind them now. "After all, I coexist with Spencer Sorrell, and you know how well we get along."

"Like the Hatfields and the McCoys," affirmed her friend.

Across the room, Jason began taking his leave. A knot of people showered him with cries of "Goodbye" and "Can't wait to see you again." Loretta's voice was among the loudest.

Patrick, who had returned from taking his phone call, escorted Jason outside. The two men seemed a bit more relaxed in each other's company than when they'd arrived.

"Let's face it, he'll be a blessing to many of the patients," Heather said. "I'm learning new techniques as quickly as I can, but this field is exploding. It'll be great to have someone like Jason to take the most difficult cases."

"You won't be rivals?" Natalie asked.

"I'm sure we can work out a satisfactory arrangement that benefits our patients," came the brisk response.

Other people departed in droves now that Jason had gone. Natalie excused herself to help clean up.

Patrick didn't return. Whatever he'd wanted, it could wait until she got back to the office. Or perhaps he hadn't been trying to get her attention at all.

PATRICK SCARCELY HEARD a word of the press conference, except to note with relief that his new infertility specialist knew how to behave himself in public. Of course, so did Spencer Sorrell.

Well, Jason was a different man. Dedicated to his work rather than to his own ego, Patrick hoped.

He couldn't give too much thought to the specialist, however, because Natalie's image kept intruding on his awareness. She was blooming, he'd realized after taking a close look at her. These past few weeks, her face had filled out a bit and her skin taken on a velvety freshness.

Was she pregnant? Was it really possible he was going to be a father?

Patrick didn't know how he felt about that. Intrigued, but alarmed, too.

Despite being a pediatrician, he'd realized years ago that he wasn't cut out for fatherhood. He was too much like his father, a lifelong workaholic.

The worst thing a man could do was fail his wife and child. During his own unsuccessful romances, Patrick had become convinced that he lacked the ability to meet a woman's deepest needs. Yet he could hardly abandon Natalie if she was carrying his child.

They had to talk. Today.

In the parking lot, he shook hands with Jason and watched him drive off in his rental car. The man zipped around a slow-moving station wagon and shot onto Bordeaux Way.

He and Jason had more in common than he'd suspected, Patrick reflected wryly: they were both impatient and intense. He wondered if either of them had weighed the cost of their obsessions. On the other hand, maybe neither of them had a choice.

He stifled an impulse to return to the conference room. There'd be too many people hanging around for him to have a private conversation with Natalie. Earlier, wrapped up in his discovery, he'd nearly approached her; then it had struck him what an inappropriate time and place this was.

Well, until she returned, Patrick needed to get back to work. He'd received a cell-phone call from the party planner, who was trying to get a permit to allow an outdoor band at the Oktoberfest. Patrick had promised to call some city officials who supported Doctors Circle.

As soon as he entered the outer office, he stopped cold. Who was this man daydreaming in Natalie's chair? Fortyish, with a long face and thinning red hair, the fellow had his feet propped on her desk as if he belonged there.

Realizing the man hadn't noticed him, Patrick reached back and rapped sharply on the door. The reaction was almost comical. The man's feet flew up, tipping him off balance, and he might have gone over backward if he hadn't grabbed the edge of the desk.

"Hey!" said the intruder. "You shouldn't sneak up on a guy."

"I was hardly sneaking. This is my office." Patrick hoped he wasn't facing an aggressive salesman. In his current mood, he might pitch the fellow out bodily. "May I help you?"

"So you're Nattie's boss," the man said. "I was waiting to have lunch with her."

"I see." Patrick made a quick mental adjustment. Not a salesman, but a...what? Friend? Brother? "Are you related to her?"

"I used to be." The fellow grinned. "I'm her husband."

"I see." Patrick supposed he ought to remove himself from the situation, since the interloper had apparently been invited. On the other hand, he'd heard that Natalie's marriage had ended unhappily five years ago. Perhaps she was being harassed. "Is she expecting you?"

"Yeah, sure." The man stood up and thrust out his hand. "I'm Ralph Winford. I guess you're Dr. Barr."

"Pleased to meet you, Mr. Winford." As they shook hands, Patrick caught a whiff of soap and, faintly, motor oil. "I didn't realize you still lived in the area."

"I get around." Ralph smiled, apparently eager to ingratiate himself. "I was living in Texas, but right now the most important thing is Nattie."

"In what sense?" Patrick asked.

"My wife is a fine woman, don't you think?" Ralph said. "I mean, to you she's just a secretary, but to me, well, I think it's wonderful that she's forgiven me after the way I behaved. I don't mind saying, I was a real mess."

What did he mean, she'd forgiven him? Natalie hadn't mentioned her ex-husband coming back into her life, yet Ralph was referring to her as his wife. Patrick wondered how long this had been going on.

Surely she wouldn't have gone to bed with him on the yacht if she'd reconciled with her former spouse. In fact, he couldn't imagine Natalie having anything to do with this scoundrel. Then again, she *had* married him once upon a time.

"She's agreed to have lunch with you?" Patrick said.

"She wouldn't want anyone else to know yet, but it's a lot more than that," Ralph said. "We were married for three years. There's ties that don't dissolve just because some judge signs a piece of paper."

"I suppose not." Since Patrick had never come close to getting married, he couldn't say if Ralph had a point.

"The one thing Nattie always wanted was children," the man rambled on. "I think it's a shame, a young woman like her ending up alone, not getting what she most wants out of life. I still care about her and deep down she still cares about me. Getting back together with her, well, it's like a dream come true."

If Natalie had reconciled with her husband, it must be his child she carried. Disappointment seared through Patrick.

Even though he knew he wasn't suited for fatherhood, he didn't want her to be pregnant by someone else. Yet he had to admit, this would explain why she hadn't wanted to continue their involvement.

When she slept with Patrick, she must have been in an unsettled mood. Had she been trying to make up her mind or acting on impulse?

There was no point in trying to understand women. He certainly couldn't figure out why a delightful person like Natalie would ally herself with an annoying fellow like this. There was no accounting for taste.

"Congratulations," Patrick said. "When your wife shows up, tell her there's no hurry. The two of you should enjoy your lunch."

"Thanks, Doc." Ralph grinned again. There was nothing to smile about, in Patrick's opinion. "I'll tell her you said so."

"I NEVER AGREED to see you." Natalie glanced anxiously at Patrick's door. She shuddered to think of her boss encountering her oily ex-husband.

"Don't worry about the doc. He said we should take our time, stay out as long as we want." Ralph looked pleased with himself.

"You met him?" she asked in dismay.

"We had a nice chat," her ex-husband said. "He liked me a lot." He smoothed down his red-orange blazer, preening like a peacock.

"Sure he did." When she'd dated Ralph years ago, Natalie had been naive enough to believe the stories he spun. It hadn't taken long after marriage to discover that, given a sympathetic or even mildly tolerant audience, he embroidered at length on his own achievements. "What did you tell him?"

"Have lunch with me and find out."

She didn't want to go. But she had to get Ralph away from this office before he did any damage.

Then she noticed the paper sack with a note, and remembered that Heather had said she was sending vitamins. "Did you read this?"

Startled, her ex-husband shook his head. From his reaction, she gathered he hadn't noticed it. Otherwise, he would certainly have snooped.

Natalie glanced at Cynthia's note. It said, "Dr. Rourke asked me to leave these for you. I'm afraid Dr. Barr noticed them. I hope this doesn't create any problems."

First prenatal vitamins showed up, then Ralph. What on earth did Patrick think was going on?

She'd have to find out later. Right now she needed to remove her ex from the premises, even at the cost of lunching with him.

By the time she was halfway through eating at a nearby hamburger joint—she and Ralph split the bill, at her insistence—she wondered if any jury in the world would convict her if she strangled him. The man had more or less announced to Patrick that the two of them were back together.

"You have a lot of nerve," she told him. "Get this through your head. I wouldn't take you back under any circumstances. If you were the last man in the—"

"I didn't figure you would." He assumed a sheepish expression. "Just figured I'd give you the opportunity."

"How kind of you." If only he hadn't shot his mouth off in front of Patrick! But then, his actions were typical of Ralph.

"You know, Nattie, I've been doing well in Texas." A change in tone alerted her that, for once, her ex-husband was talking straight. "I've been on the wagon for three years, and I'm head mechanic at my garage."

"Good for you." She decided not to repeat her request that he pay back the debts he'd stuck her with. That could come later. "Now tell me the reason you decided to invade my life again."

"I want to open my own shop." Ralph downed another bite of hamburger and talked with his mouth full.

"I've found a place I can lease cheap and I've got customers who like my work."

"You need a loan," Natalie summed up.

"An investment," he corrected. "In a few years it would pay off big."

"Yeah, sure." Even if the garage was a success, she figured her ex-husband would hire a creative book-keeper to hide the profits.

"Okay, a loan," said Ralph. "We'll work out a payment schedule and everything."

Just like Candy. The money she'd given her sister for liposuction was no doubt gone with the wind. A loan to Ralph would suffer the same fate. "Are you offering collateral?"

"Collateral?" he asked.

"Never mind." Even if she could foreclose on a garage in Texas, what would she do with it? "I don't have enough money to lend you any, and if I did, I wouldn't."

"Nattie, I'll pay back the rest of what I owe you, too. We'll write that into the deal."

"There is no deal, Ralph."

"You don't actually need to lend me the money," he said. "You could guarantee my loan with a bank. You always have great credit."

"Which you'd be happy to ruin for me." Natalie got to her feet. "If you come to my office again, I'll swear out a restraining order against you. The same goes for my apartment. I wish you luck with your enterprise, but you'll have to find someone else to foot the bill."

He stared, on the verge of anger, and then he shrugged. "Guess I'm not surprised. You can't blame a guy for trying."

He was good with cars, Natalie reflected as she left

the restaurant. She sincerely hoped he would do well with his business. Any further involvement on her part, however, was out of the question.

She didn't delude herself that the man would give up this easily. Whether it was by phone or e-mail, he'd no doubt make a pest of himself until he got the message through his thick skull that she wasn't going to buckle.

She only wished she could find out exactly what he'd told Patrick. Knowing Ralph, she had a feeling there was more to it than he'd confessed.

Chapter Seven

Impossible. He wasn't jealous of that unpleasant man who used to be married to Natalie, was he?

Sitting at his desk, Patrick ran his fingers through his hair and tried again to concentrate on the copy for a brochure about Doctors Circle's charity programs. His eyes refused to make sense of the words.

He kept seeing Natalie, aglow in the early-evening light as she lay beside him aboard the *Melissa*. She hadn't held back in any way. There'd been no hint of conflicting loyalties.

Yet she must have slept with him and her ex-husband within a few weeks of each other, which explained why she was pregnant in spite of their precautions. The knowledge troubled Patrick, yet he refused to judge her. He didn't know all the facts.

Grimly he returned his attention to editing the brochure copy. Half an hour later, he heard a familiar rustling in the outer office and felt a whisper of air through the open doorway. His skin prickled in anticipation.

Natalie tapped on the frame. "Excuse me."

"Yes?" Patrick looked up. Unquestionably, she had

blossomed these past few weeks, he thought. Even her blond hair looked fuller.

"My ex-husband has a big mouth," she said. "And there's something else we need to discuss. Those vitamins Cynthia left on my desk."

"It's none of my business." He was glad to hear no sign of tension in his voice.

"It certainly *is* your business." Natalie's eyes flashed blue fire.

"I hope you won't be leaving your job." He hoped she wasn't going to move away with her husband. Patrick needed her too much.

"That never crossed my mind," she said.

"Good." He took a deep breath. "Look, this could be a messy situation and none of us needs that."

"Are you saying you want to stay out of the picture?" Natalie asked, sounding surprised. "For the sake of the center, I presume."

"For everyone's sake." Beneath the desk, Patrick's hands formed fists. He didn't know how much longer he could go on acting magnanimous when every instinct urged him to grab her, throw her over his shoulder like a caveman and head for the hills.

"Let me get this straight," Natalie said. "You're aware that I'm going to have a baby?"

He nodded.

"That doesn't bother you?"

"Your ex-husband made it clear you'd wanted a child for a long time," Patrick said. "I think it's wonderful for the two of you."

"The two of us?" she muttered. "He said that?"

"I hope he'll be a good father." Patrick didn't mean to express doubts about the man, but surely she nurtured a few of her own. "The more I've seen of children, the more I recognize how much they need their fathers. I'd make a lousy one, as you've probably noticed. I'm too impatient and too absorbed in my work. But you'll be a wonderful mother, and I hope your ex-husband—"

He stopped himself. He had no right to speculate about what kind of parent Ralph would make.

"You're pleased for me?" Natalie asked with what sounded like amazement.

"Absolutely."

"I see." She waited, but he had nothing more to say. Finally she went out and closed the door.

Patrick sensed that he'd disappointed her. Yet surely she didn't expect him to challenge Ralph to a duel. Scalpels at twenty paces?

More likely, she was glad his attitude was so reasonable. Whatever concerns she might have, they would disappear when she held that baby in her arms and saw Ralph's expression of...of...

It was impossible to picture that man looking anything but smug. Patrick hoped for Natalie's sake that he was wrong.

NATALIE DIDN'T KNOW which man made her angrier, Ralph or Patrick. One was a manipulative liar, and the other seemed relieved to get her off his hands.

Although the vitamin pills had been sitting on the desk, Natalie didn't think Ralph had guessed that she was pregnant, since he hadn't mentioned it to her. More likely, he'd been yammering away in a confused attempt to impress Patrick. In fact, it had to be the latter, because her ex-husband wouldn't have suggested even in passing that she take him back if he knew she was carrying another man's child.

As for Patrick, he assumed she'd known he didn't want to be a father. Well, no, she hadn't. Quite the opposite. Based on her own observations, her boss was terrific with children.

She sat down behind her desk, her mind racing. In a way, Ralph had handed her the perfect out. She no longer had to worry that, once Patrick learned of her pregnancy, he would know he was the father.

She'd believed he might offer to marry her, and then she'd have to admit to lying on her application. That would risk losing both him and her career.

Instead, Patrick was delighted to be off the hook, and perhaps Natalie should be, too. What was the point of telling him the truth now and burdening him with a baby he didn't want?

Because he deserves to know his child. Because this child deserves to know its father.

Natalie wanted to do the right thing. But what was right in this case?

Patrick didn't want the baby, and neither he nor Doctors Circle needed a scandal. If everyone thought the baby was Ralph's, Natalie might have to endure a few snide remarks from Spencer Sorrell, but she was used to that. As for Ralph himself, he'd be long gone before her pregnancy began to show.

As an employer, Patrick would stand by her. Also, he might not want to be a full-time father, but he loved being an uncle, so perhaps he'd spend at least a little time with their child. As for day care, one thing Natalie knew about her mother: Angie loved babies, and she loved grandbabies most of all.

It was almost too easy. She could get away with it. Of course, she'd never be able to hold Patrick in her arms again, but that was beginning to seem less and less likely, anyway. Not that it didn't hurt—it hurt like fire. But she could bear it if she had to.

Natalie was lost in thought when she registered the sound of heels clicking toward her from the hallway. Heather stepped into the room. She clutched a slim envelope. "Hi, Nat. Is Patrick in?"

"Sure." Natalie was about to buzz him on the intercom when he emerged with a couple of letters for her to mail.

"Heather!" he said. "I'm glad you're here. I want to apologize for not notifying you in advance that we were hiring Dr. Carmichael. I should have done so out of professional courtesy."

Heather's sprinkling of freckles rippled as she blinked a couple of times. "Don't worry about it. We have something else to discuss." She extended the envelope.

Patrick accepted it. "Please, come inside." He led the way.

Natalie hoped nothing was wrong with her friend. Sometimes it seemed like working at a medical center meant dealing with one crisis after another.

She picked up a stack of résumés HR had forwarded from applicants for the job of Jason Carmichael's secretary. An advertisement in Sunday's newspaper had brought in several dozen faxes, and more applications would no doubt arrive by mail.

The first résumé came from a young woman just out of high school, the second from a homemaker returning to work after a long hiatus. The good doctor would eat either of them alive, she thought regretfully.

She kept searching. Sooner or later, Ms. Perfect would turn up.

PATRICK FROWNED as he reread the letter. Judging by the typos, Heather must have dashed it off in a hurry after the press conference.

She was asking for two months' leave from her job, citing undisclosed personal reasons. The leave was to begin at the beginning of October, a mere week away.

"Two months is a long time," he said. "And this is short notice."

"I've never done anything like this before and I'm sorry, but it has to be this way." Heather, usually open and good-natured, sat ramrod straight in her chair and failed to elaborate.

"You must be fully booked with patients," Patrick said.

"That concerns me as much as it does you, believe me, but there is a solution." She clasped her hands in her lap. "As you'll recall, we've got Rob Sentinel joining the staff this week."

The demand for obstetrical services had been increasing steadily. To help deal with it, Patrick had hired an additional doctor with training in both normal and high-risk pregnancies.

Rob Sentinel was a gifted young physician who'd chosen to relocate from New York to Southern California. Although he would be acquiring his own clients as time went on, Rob should be able to take over Heather's appointments for the next two months.

"Are you sure you want to do this?" Patrick asked.

"You know how much your patients depend on you, and some of your infertility procedures will have to be postponed."

Heather's expressive face flushed guiltily. "You don't have to tell me that. I wish it could be otherwise, but it can't."

"You could force my hand," Patrick said, "but I hope you'll give me a day or so to consider this." He hesitated to raise the next issue, but it was unavoidable. "This doesn't have anything to do with Dr. Carmichael joining us, does it?"

"Of course not." Her mouth pursed in irritation. "A few minutes ago I received a telephone call about a personal matter that requires my immediate presence. That's all I care to disclose."

"I see." But he didn't. If Heather had a sick relative, why not say so? It was hard to imagine what other sort of emergency required such extended leave. "Please bear with me. I need to make sure we can meet our obligations to our clients. Unless you or someone in your family is ill, there could be legal ramifications."

"I can postpone my departure for another week, but that's pushing it." Heather's lips clamped tightly.

"I'll get back to you as quickly as I can." Patrick stood, and they shook hands. "In the future I trust you'll let me know if you have any problems with our new infertility chief."

"Believe me, this request has nothing to do with him or anyone else at Doctors Circle." Heather didn't meet his eyes as she spoke, though. Her evasiveness was so uncharacteristic that Patrick became all the more uneasy.

That afternoon he made certain that there was room

on Dr. Sentinel's schedule for all of Dr. Rourke's clients and that they could be notified promptly. Still, having a doctor depart suddenly for unspecified reasons was unsettling.

Despite Heather's denial, she *had* asked for leave right after the press conference. Perhaps she'd wanted to head the infertility clinic herself and planned to spend her time off seeking a new job. Patrick had assumed because she didn't submit an application that she wasn't interested, but perhaps that had been an error. He would hate to lose such a fine doctor.

It was a relief when Natalie, after dropping the afternoon mail on his desk, broached the subject herself. "Heather says she's taking two months off. Is there a problem I can help with?"

Patrick shook his head wearily. "She didn't give a reason. I wish I could be sure it isn't a reaction to our new infertility director."

"That occurred to me, too." Natalie eased into a chair. It felt good to be talking things over with her. Patrick wasn't ready to think about the fact that she, too, would be going on leave in seven or eight months.

"I'd hate to take a hard line with her, but she does have an employment contract," he said. "Mostly, I feel bad for her patients."

"They'll adjust," Natalie said. "Hey, I'm not thrilled about having to see a new doctor myself, but at least Heather should be back for my delivery."

Ralph would be here, too, Patrick realized. He pictured the man's watery eyes beaming with satisfaction, his hands smelling of motor oil as he coached Natalie through labor or, more likely, yakked with the nurses while she suffered. How could she stand the fellow?

Patrick tore his mind away. "I promised to get back to Dr. Rourke as soon as possible."

"Do you want my advice?" Natalie asked.

"Sure."

"Trust her," she said.

As usual, his secretary had cut to the crux of the matter. Much as Patrick felt responsible for all that happened at Doctors Circle, he couldn't run everyone's lives. He had to believe that Heather was obeying her own conscience and not acting out of spite.

"I'll do that," he said. "Her leave is granted."

"You'll tell her today?" Natalie asked.

"I'm making the call right now." She'd be pleased to get such a quick response, he thought as he reached for the phone.

"DID HEATHER SAY anything to you?" Natalie asked Amy on Friday afternoon as they sipped coffee in the courtyard. It wasn't easy to schedule their breaks at the same time, but for once they'd managed.

"Not a word about why she's going on leave." Amy's dark hair was, as usual late in the day, struggling to escape its French braid. "I can't imagine what she's up to."

Natalie had done her best all week not to pry. She'd seen Heather several times while ferrying paperwork to her, and was doubly intrigued when she noticed a simmering excitement in her friend's expression. "Whatever it is, she's really eager. Nervous, too."

"An old love?" Amy speculated. "I don't see why she'd need two months, though."

"Maybe she's going to meet him abroad," Natalie said.

"That might take a few weeks, not months." The dark-haired woman sipped her mocha through a straw. "Unless they're going on something intensive like an archaeological expedition together or whatever."

"I doubt it. They'd have had to plan ahead."

The two of them sat trying to figure out explanations and not coming up with any. At the fountain, a little girl tossed in a penny, scrunched up her face and made a wish. A bird landed near her feet and pecked at crumbs.

"Speaking of secrets," Amy said, "the word's spreading that you're pregnant. People are taking bets about the father's identity. Not that I would stoop so low."

Natalie wasn't surprised word had gotten out. A lot of people who knew her must have seen her records and lab reports in the course of their work. Although violations of patient confidentiality were grounds for dismissal, she had to admit that if she'd really wanted to ensure privacy, she could have gone to a doctor at another site. Anyway, her colleagues were sure to notice her condition before long.

"They're wasting their time betting," she said. "This is my baby. I'm going to have it alone and raise it by myself. Well, with some help from my mom, I hope."

Amy whistled. "You're one tough cookie. Count on me to help, too." Cautiously she added, "Did you tell the father?"

"Sort of." Natalie picked up her cup. "Time to get back to work. Doing anything special tonight?"

Amy scrunched up her empty cup and scored a perfect hit into a trash container. "I'm taking my seventeen-year-old cousin to a baseball game, trying to broaden her perspective. All she ever thinks about are boys and clothes and her hair.''

''They have boys at baseball games,'' Natalie said as she dropped her trash in the basket. ''Clothes and hair, too.''

''At least I'm getting her out of the mall,'' Amy said. ''What are you doing tonight?''

''Eating dinner at my mother's,'' Natalie said, ''and breaking the big news.''

''Good luck!''

''This should be interesting.'' She hadn't yet figured out how she was going to keep the father's identity a secret from Angie.

IN A CROCK-POT, Angie had fixed a roast doused with beer. ''I ran out of sherry,'' she explained as she fished out the succulent meat with a slotted spoon. Since the alcohol would have evaporated, Natalie figured it was safe for her to eat.

''Smells great to me.'' Clovis slapped paper plates around the table.

To her relief, only the three of them were present. Although Candy mooched off her mother as often as possible, Natalie suspected her sister was avoiding her for fear of a demand that she start repaying her debt. According to Angie, the liposuction was scheduled in a few days.

The meal consisted of the meat, assorted rolls that Angie pulled out of the freezer and microwaved, and a salad Natalie had brought. Angie talked at length about the dolls she was making for Doctors Circle.

"That boss of yours is a peach," she concluded. "Is he married?"

"He's married to his work," Natalie said.

"Not so married he couldn't carry your shopping bag on his day off," her mother noted.

"Don't start matchmaking," Clovis said. "Next thing you know, she'll be having a baby."

It was the perfect opening. Natalie tried to find the right words, and failed.

"I'd like to have a grandbaby around here." Angie covered her salad with ranch dressing. "Alana's got two in Oregon, but she gets short-tempered every time I mention visiting, and anyhow, it rains too much up there for my taste. Then there's Max in Las Vegas— we ought to go visit him and check out that casino where he works. His wife had number four last month. Did you know that?"

"I sent a gift certificate," Natalie said. "I couldn't imagine what baby stuff they wouldn't already have."

"There's a big crafts fair coming up in Vegas." Clovis leaned back in his chair and stretched out his jean-clad legs. There were holes in the knees, which didn't seem to embarrass him. "We could combine business with pleasure."

Angie's voluminous pink hair rippled as she nodded. "I haven't heard from my son Bill in two, three years. I wonder if he's still in the navy and if he's got kids now, too."

Natalie couldn't wait any longer. "Well, you're going to have another one."

Both her companions studied her. "Another what?" Clovis said.

"Grandbaby?" Angie asked. "You've got a bun in the oven?"

"I'm due in May," Natalie said.

Her mother flung her arms around her. "I can't believe it! The father's that wonderful Dr. Barr, isn't it?"

A word from Angie to anyone at the Doctors Circle gift shop and the whole staff would hear it. Including Patrick. "Maybe not. It might be Ralph."

Clovis nearly fell off his chair. "You slept with Ralph?"

How could she even pretend she'd been that foolish? Natalie admonished herself. "Well, no."

Clovis squinted at her. "Then how could he be the father?"

"It's kind of hard to explain."

"I guess so," Angie said.

"Please trust me about this," Natalie said. "The father's identity needs to remain a secret right now, okay?"

They both nodded, although her mother did so reluctantly. However, soon they were engrossed in a discussion of what to name it, and the subject of the father's identity was left for another day.

EARLY ON SATURDAY Patrick sat at the desk in his upstairs bedroom and reviewed the menu for the Oktoberfest, which was a week away. The guests would be sampling sausages and sauerkraut, hamburgers and German-style potato salad, several kinds of imported beer and non-alcoholic beer.

Through the window, a movement caught his eye. In the pool, his sister, Bernie, was swimming laps. Through a screen of tree branches, he glimpsed her white-capped head and the sleek red-and-black of her suit.

He turned to the song list for the oompah band, now that a permit had been secured. The melodies were old German favorites that never lost their appeal, with a few Viennese waltzes and Polish polkas thrown in.

Instinctively he glanced out the window again. Through the branches, he caught a couple of jerky, thrashing movements. He waited a few seconds, but they didn't resolve into smooth strokes, nor did Bernie reappear.

Shoeless and wearing only a T-shirt and jeans, Patrick raced downstairs and across the lawn. His heart pounded as he prayed he was in time to save his sister.

Chapter Eight

Time dragged, as if Patrick were running in slow motion. Far too many seconds passed before he reached the pool and spotted his sister struggling in the deep end, losing the battle to keep her head above water.

He dived into the pool. As he pushed off from the edge, his ankle twisted and pain stabbed through him. Ignoring it, he kicked hard toward his sister and grabbed her.

She came to the surface gasping and choking. In a panic, she clutched at his arms, putting them both in danger of sinking. After wrenching free, Patrick positioned himself behind her and towed her to the edge of the pool.

She clung to the rim, coughing harshly. He hoisted himself onto the concrete, put weight on his injured ankle and pitched forward in agony.

"What—?" Bernie couldn't finish the sentence.

"It's my ankle." On his knees, he braced himself, making sure to keep his hurt leg clear, and reached for her hand. "Come on out of there."

"I'll see if I can." She made a couple of feeble attempts at leaving the water unaided, then gave up and took his hand. With Patrick tugging, Bernie landed smack on the concrete. "Ow!" She inspected her skin. "I scraped my leg."

"I guess we're both goners," he teased, sitting beside her. "We better call the paramedics."

She tried to answer and coughed a few times before her throat cleared. "Sorry—I didn't mean to complain. Thanks for saving my life."

"Are you sure you're all right? We nearly lost you!" Patrick reached over and hugged her. Her skin felt chilled and she was trembling.

"I'm not in shock. Just shook up and a little cold."

Taking her wrist, he checked her pulse. It was strong and steady. He made a mental note to keep an eye on her, anyway. "I'm glad I spotted you right away. You really scared me."

"Mike always told me it was foolish to swim alone." His sister made a wry face. "I promise to bring a partner along from now on."

"What happened?"

"Stomach cramps," she said. "They were like a vise. I haven't been squeezed that hard since my kids were born."

"You shouldn't swim right after eating." Patrick could hear his mother's voice giving the same warning years ago.

"I didn't," his sister said. "Kip had the cramps yesterday for about an hour. I thought it was food poisoning, but it must be one of those short-term viruses."

"Do you feel sick?" he asked.

"Just crampy. It's getting better already. How's your ankle?"

Tentatively, Patrick pressed on it. A lightning bolt of pain shocked the breath from him.

Bernie regarded her brother with concern. "You're worse off than I am."

"It's no big deal," he said. "You're the one who needs to get checked."

"You need that ankle x-rayed," his sister said.

"It's fine."

"Doctors always think they're impervious to harm," she answered tartly. "Come on. I'm driving you to a hospital, and not one that specializes in pregnant women, either."

ON SATURDAY MORNING, Natalie answered a tap at her door to find Candy standing there with a box of doughnuts. "Congratulations. Mom says you're knocked up."

"Come in." Natalie ushered her sister into the living room and went to fetch two coffee mugs, one shaped like a rabbit and the other decorated with images of Bugs Bunny. Candy, she knew, took her coffee black. In deference to her own condition, Natalie added milk to hers.

"You ought to cut down on the caffeine now that you're preggers." On the coffee table, Candy opened the box, releasing a sugary scent.

"I'm planning to. Any day now," Natalie said.

From her purse, her sister took a check and set it on the table. It was the check Natalie had given her for surgery. "I'm not having the liposuction."

"Why not?" She refrained from cheering her sister's decision. The surest way to antagonize Candy was to say I-told-you-so.

"They gave the modeling job to someone else." Candy clasped her hands in her lap.

"That must be why you're indulging in sweets,

too.'' Natalie handed her a mug and sat down, folding away the check.

"Yeah. Also, I'm giving up acting." In the morning light, her sister looked younger than her thirty-three years, but apparently not young enough for Hollywood. "I'm giving up that crummy low-paying hotel desk job, too. I got hired as a tour guide."

"What kind of tour guide?" Natalie had a hard time picturing her sister wearing a uniform and patiently pointing out the sights to a busload of noisy visitors.

"I show small groups of businesspeople around," she said. "Mostly men."

"But you don't speak any foreign languages."

"The people I work with speak English," Candy said. "I already took out my first group, with a supervisor. You wouldn't believe how many good-looking guys there were! And I'll bet some of them are rich, too."

"Candy!" Natalie had to choose between giving her sister a shake and nabbing the only chocolate doughnut. She chose the doughnut. "You can't possibly believe you're going to land a husband!"

Candy's blue eyes took on a dreamy look that her sister knew too well. "You never know. I might meet Mr. Right."

"You're more likely to meet Mr. Married."

"I can take care of myself," Candy said. "Right now you're the one who needs help. Who's the father? And don't give me that guff about Ralph. You wouldn't touch him with a ten-foot pole."

"The father is out of the picture," Natalie said. "Case closed."

Her sister opened her mouth as if to argue, then apparently thought better of it. "I guess if you can accept my flirting with tourists," she said, "I can let you have a mystery lover."

"Fair enough." Natalie's second-choice doughnut was lemon-filled. It tasted fabulous. "As soon as I finish my coffee, I've got to head over to the office. I should have been there earlier, but it took me forever to wake up this morning. Pregnant women sleep deeply."

"It's Saturday," Candy reminded her.

"There's more work than I can finish in five days." Including additional résumés to review for Dr. Carmichael, Natalie reflected.

The phone rang. When she answered, she was surprised to find Bernie on the line. "Patrick's been injured," his sister said without preamble.

Natalie's chest constricted as she pictured a devastating automobile accident. "How badly?"

Candy looked up, a question in her eyes. Natalie couldn't signal to her, not now when her heart hung in the balance.

"He sprained his ankle rescuing me in the pool," Bernie said. "We're at the hospital. He's getting it wrapped right now."

"I'm glad it wasn't serious." Relief flooded through Natalie. He was safe, even if somewhat the worse for wear. "Are you all right?"

"I'm fine, but as for Patrick, when I say sprained, I mean big time," Bernie said. "This is the kind of sprain that puts people on crutches and lays them up in front of the TV. My brother's refusing to take it easy, though. He says he's got too much work."

That was typical of the man. "I can drive him to work until his ankle gets better. Don't worry, it's not inconvenient, since he lives a block from the office."

In response to her sister's gesture of curiosity, Natalie scribbled on a notepad: "My boss sprained his ankle." Candy read it and shrugged, as if disappointed that the news wasn't more dramatic.

"It's absolutely, totally against doctors' orders for him to limp any farther than the kitchen," Bernie said. "He can't even climb stairs, so we'll have to convert his bedroom into an office."

"I can bring his work over, if he'd like." In the age of e-mail and faxes, Patrick could operate from home for a few days.

Candy strolled to the window and frowned at something through the gauzy curtains. Faintly, Natalie heard footsteps scuffing across the concrete below her apartment.

"Thanks, but..." Bernie let out a low cough. "Sorry, I'm still a little congested from the water. The point is, I can't leave my brother by himself. What if there's an emergency? I don't want him to be alone, and the housekeeper only comes in two days a week."

Patrick was as far from helpless as any man Natalie had ever met. "He's strong and he's resourceful."

"He's also pigheaded. Don't encourage him in this tough-guy attitude," Bernie said. "He got hurt saving me, so he's my responsibility. I can't abandon him, but I hate to stay away from my family."

Natalie began to suspect where this conversation was headed. "You're not suggesting I move in with him, are you?"

"Only for a few days. You'd have to be at the estate a lot this week to help set up for the Oktoberfest, anyway, wouldn't you?" Bernie said.

Patrick's sister never took no for an answer, but how

could Natalie stay at the Barr house? That would mean seeing Patrick day and night.

It was dangerous. Exhilarating. Unthinkable.

"Hire a nurse," she said. "She'll do a better job of caring for his ankle, and she won't excite gossip."

"I don't want a nurse. A nurse won't watch over him the way you or I would," Bernie said. "If you say no, it has to be me. Think of my two poor children. Think of my lonely husband." Her tone was only half-joking.

"Ralph's coming up the stairs," Candy said.

Natalie clamped her hand over the phone. "Tell me you're joking!" Then she heard his unmistakable shuffling footsteps.

"He's bearing flowers." Her sister shuddered. "He isn't really the father, is he?"

"Of course not!"

"I'm not sure I heard you correctly," Bernie said over the phone. "I thought you said 'of course not,' but that doesn't sound right."

"I was talking to my sister about something else," Natalie explained.

"Good. Then you'll do it?"

"It wouldn't be right for me to stay there." From outside she heard Ralph humming as his fingers made a skittering noise across the door. Humming, for heaven's sake, as if certain she'd cave in and give him whatever he wanted!

Natalie knew she could seek a restraining order, as she'd threatened, but it would be easier simply to disappear for a few days. Surely he couldn't be away from Texas for very long.

Besides, she didn't like to think of Bernie having to leave her husband and kids, even for a short time.

Worse, she might bring the boys along, and the swimming pool wasn't fenced. If one of the kids drowned, Natalie would never forgive herself.

"Nattie, sweetheart! Let me in!" sang Ralph.

Candy opened the door, snatched the flowers, smacked him over the head with them and slammed the door in his face. Then she burst out laughing.

"I'll be back!" Ralph called through the screened window. "You can't hide forever."

"Bernie?" Natalie said into the phone. "I'll do it."

"Thank you a million times. We'll meet you at the house," Patrick's sister said.

IF HIS ANKLE hadn't been throbbing mightily in spite of the painkiller he'd taken, Patrick would have been furious with Bernie. He didn't need a caretaker. He certainly didn't want to inconvenience Natalie, and he loathed the likelihood that her smarmy ex-husband would come calling, maybe even expect to spend the nights with her.

"You shouldn't have asked her without consulting me," he told his sister as she parked in front of his house.

"Who else was I going to ask?" she demanded, and came around to help him out of the car.

"I can manage fine by myself," he muttered as she opened the door, referring both to the specific task of removing himself from her car and to the general matter of surviving the next few days.

"Ever used a crutch before?" she demanded.

"When I had surgery on my knee back in college," he said.

"You're not twenty years old anymore," she persisted.

"I'm in better shape now than I was then," he answered grumpily. It wasn't true, but saying it gave his spirits a boost.

It had been foolish to dive off the edge of the pool without paying attention to where he placed his feet. He of all people should have known better, Patrick chided himself. Nevertheless, he'd saved Bernie, and that was what really mattered.

He swung his injured right ankle out of the car, and pivoted to put his weight on the left. He performed the unaccustomed maneuver awkwardly. Then with one hand on the car door and the other gripping his crutch, Patrick hauled himself upright. He nearly lost his balance, instinctively put down his right foot and let out a colorful curse he'd learned years ago from a diving coach.

"Gee, I thought I'd forgotten that one," he said.

"I like it," Bernie joked. "I'll use it on Mike the next time he's late for dinner."

"Don't let the boys hear you," Patrick warned.

"As if!" she said. "Now get moving, Mr. Tough Guy."

Clinging to the tattered remnants of his pride, Patrick hobbled to the front steps. There he confronted his first true obstacle. Although there were only two of them, they loomed like Mount Everest.

He was wondering whether any carpenters might be available on a Saturday to install a ramp, when Natalie's green hatchback zipped down the driveway and halted next to Bernie's car. For a moment, with the sun glinting off her windshield, he couldn't see if anyone was with her.

The last thing Patrick wanted was for Ralph to come strutting over here while he was in this condition. For some reason, the fellow roused his primal male instincts, the ones that made him want to punch another guy in the nose for even looking at Natalie.

She got out alone, then hauled a suitcase from the back seat. Moving with an ease Patrick could only envy, she reached him and set down her luggage. "Can I help?"

"Tarzan here can swing from the trees all by himself," Bernie said tartly.

"Yes, but can he walk up stairs?" Natalie asked. "Here, lean on me."

She inserted herself beneath Patrick's left arm. Almonds and honey, he registered, getting a whiff of her skin, and wondered if she'd brought her scented soap with her. For the next few days, she'd be living in his house, showering upstairs from him, all sleek and lovely...

And in light of his injury, that meant she might as well be taking a shower a thousand miles away. He gritted his teeth and, between Natalie and the crutch, managed to clear the steps.

"You're good at helping," Bernie said. "You seem to know what to do."

"My mother broke her leg in a car accident last year," Natalie said. "I got a lot of experience."

"I'll be off, then. Mike has a golf game in forty-five minutes and I need to relieve him of the kids," she said. "Thanks again for scooping me out of the deep end, bro."

"My pleasure." He watched her trot to her car, then unlocked the door and escorted Natalie inside.

In the foyer Patrick suddenly noticed how big the space was and how slippery the marble looked. Despite his appetite, it took a moment to summon the willpower to hobble across it toward the kitchen.

The sunny room, located at the back of the house, overlooked the bluffs and the sea. With generous cabinets and counter space, a center island and a round table, it had always been the emotional center of the house.

Natalie didn't chatter the way Bernie did or offer to help when it wasn't needed. She moved calmly into the kitchen and, without waiting to be shown around, opened the refrigerator. "I'll bet you'd like some lunch."

"I'm starved," Patrick admitted as he lowered himself into a chair. "I didn't think I needed anyone around, but trying to fix a meal right now would be a real challenge."

"My mother said using crutches made her arms and shoulders ache," Natalie said.

"I work out with weights, which helps," he said. "But I suppose there'll be a few twinges." If some of his muscles were already aching, he didn't intend to mention it.

Besides, the pain was subsiding. The pill must be having a delayed effect, because a sense of well-being replaced Patrick's tension.

He found himself contemplating Natalie's delightful shape with lazy lustfulness as she stood fixing sandwiches at the counter. White shorts clung to her shapely rear as she faced away from him, and when she turned to reach for a cutting board, he noticed how her maroon knit top emphasized the fullness of her bustline.

If he crossed the room and took her in his arms, he could catch her off guard. He knew the way Natalie would turn and gaze up at him with her lips parted, how she'd press her breasts against his chest...

Cross the room? Take her in his arms? He'd fall flat on his face if he tried, Patrick reflected unhappily. On the other hand, if she came over here...

He shook his head, trying to clear it. The medication must be affecting his judgment or his memory, maybe both. Natalie belonged to another man. Even if she didn't, they'd both agreed not to repeat their impulsive behavior on the yacht.

"I hope bologna is all right," she said, setting a plate in front of him.

"For the mood I'm in, bologna suits me perfectly," he said.

The medicine was taking hold with a vengeance. By the time they finished the meal, Patrick had to fight not to doze off at the table. With Natalie's help, he made it to the couch in the den and fell asleep as soon as his head touched the cushions.

WHILE HE NAPPED Natalie made a quick trip to the office to pick up some correspondence. Her boss probably wouldn't be able to respond to it today, but she had no doubt he'd snap back tomorrow.

It was rare to see him so vulnerable. In the kitchen his amber eyes had taken on a soft glint and he'd smiled easily at her. Faced with his boyish appeal, Natalie's body had tingled with forbidden longing.

This was what she'd feared, that close contact would revive their attraction. Thank goodness the painkiller had put him to sleep.

She was even tempted to import Ralph just to keep a distance between them. Well, not seriously tempted. It was a possibility in case she got desperate, though.

When she returned to the house, she found him still asleep in the den. Remembering Bernie's comment about fixing a bedroom downstairs, Natalie went into his office.

In the wood-paneled room, a faintly smoky smell—no doubt left from his father's era—mingled with the leather scent of the large sofa. Although the desk and file cabinet looked old-fashioned, they accommodated a computer and fax machine.

A ceiling-high bookcase held rows of medical texts, volumes on management and finance, and an eclectic assortment of books from the Bible to recent thrillers. Tan vertical blinds shaded a window that faced the front of the house.

The only decoration was a large, formal photograph of Joe and Lottie Barr with a younger Patrick and Bernie. She guessed that it had been shot about ten years ago.

Natalie tried to imagine taking a formal picture of her own family. There had never been a point at which everyone could be captured, of course, because Angie's three husbands had come and gone over the years. It wouldn't have worked, anyway, because her brothers and sisters were usually feuding with one another or with their mother.

This room and this house, much as she loved them, were a reminder of the vast distance between Patrick and her. Natalie loved her family, but she knew their messy lives had nothing in common with the Barrs.

Her sister was a husband-hunting tour guide, for heaven's sake! Finn Sorrell would sneer if he heard that, and no doubt he *would* hear. Despite its sophistication, Serene Beach was still a small town.

Natalie opened the couch into a bed. There were

sheets in place, and she found a blanket and pillow in the closet. The housekeeper certainly did a good job of being prepared.

She was straightening the bed when Patrick shambled in, his hair rumpled and his T-shirt plastered against his chest. Instead of a hospital administrator, he looked more like a rough-hewn hero ready to sweep her off her feet—if he could manage it in spite of the crutch.

With an appreciative gleam in his eye, he surveyed her shorts and knit top. Whatever medication Patrick had taken, it must have loosened his inhibitions.

"I made the bed for you," she said unnecessarily.

"How about for us?" The words came out a little slurred.

"I'm sleeping on the second floor," Natalie reminded him, refusing to take offense while he was in this state.

Patrick leaned against the desk, a smile playing across his mouth. "There's a whirlpool bath up there. A soak would do my ankle a world of good."

"Too bad you don't have an elevator."

"We can work this out together," he proposed.

"Climbing the stairs or taking a bath?"

"Both." He reached for her, missed by several feet and nearly lost his balance. "Darn. My depth perception is off."

"By about a mile," Natalie agreed. "Your judgment is impaired, too."

"An impaired judgment used to be taken as a sign that the gods had touched you," he said.

"In which ancient civilization was that? Or perhaps it was your college fraternity?" Patrick had never looked so carefree or so openly admiring, Natalie thought with guilty enjoyment as she awaited his reply.

"Both," he announced. "Now, I have something important to say to you."

She felt a spurt of alarm. "Maybe you ought to wait until you're fully in control of yourself."

"But then I won't say it," Patrick replied. "I'm awfully stiff-necked most of the time, aren't I."

"Your behavior fits your job," she said.

"Then I must have a stiff-necked job." He edged toward her, bearing down on the crutch. Clearly he hadn't yet mastered the knack of using it, because he stumbled and plopped onto the edge of the bed.

Natalie backed away. "Whatever you have to say, if it's important, it'll come out eventually."

"Eventually is too far off." Patrick paused. "It's about what's-his-name. Your husband."

"My ex." Natalie hated to speak Ralph's name here in Patrick's house.

"He's not good enough for you," he told her gravely. "I understand about your wanting a child. But you deserve someone more responsible. And less odious."

"You found him odious?" She didn't bother to hide her amusement. "He made a strong impression in a short amount of time, I see."

"You should let me pick someone for you," Patrick said. "Someone more like me."

The conversation had become absurd. "Let me guess. A doctor."

"A man of standing in the community." Patrick kept pausing, as if his thoughts were drifting away, but each time he pulled them back. "Someone who'll take proper care of you and your child."

"He wouldn't have brown hair and eyes, would he?" Natalie asked.

"The color of his hair is irrelevant," he said. "Or whether he has any hair at all."

"You aren't thinking of Spencer Sorrell!" She threw up her hands in mock horror.

"Absolutely not. I'm speaking theoretically." Patrick rubbed the corner of his eye. "What were we talking about?"

"About the fact that you need another nap," Natalie said.

"That isn't a bad idea." Dropping the crutch, he stretched out. Within minutes, his lids closed and his breathing grew regular.

She allowed herself to linger for several minutes, luxuriating in the sight of his handsome face relaxed in sleep. If only she dared lie down beside him...

But she didn't, Natalie thought, and went to fetch her suitcase.

Chapter Nine

In his dream Patrick searched frantically through an attic he'd never seen before. There was something he'd forgotten, some vital item he'd misplaced, and it had to be here.

If only he could remember what it was, he'd have a better chance of finding it among so many trunks and boxes. He pawed through a stack of swim-team jackets, a pile of college textbooks and some of his father's invention sketches. What was he missing? What had he lost?

Someone moved in the back of the attic. When Patrick focused, he saw it was Joe Barr, his face thin from working too hard and eating too little. His father, that was who he'd been looking for, but why?

He awoke with a start into late-afternoon light. The dream vanished, leaving only a sense of disquiet.

He blinked and absorbed the fact that he had fallen asleep in his father's office. Was Dad working late again? He was so rarely at home that sometimes his little boy came downstairs and waited for hours just to see him.

A throb in his right ankle brought the present rushing back in. Dad wasn't lost; he'd died five years ago. Being in his old office must have affected Patrick's subconscious mind and spurred the dream.

It came to him that he'd been holding a disjointed conversation with Natalie before he dozed off. Whatever he'd said, it had probably sounded idiotic.

Since his ankle was hurting, he could tell that the painkiller was wearing off. Patrick decided not to take another pill until bedtime, so that, with luck, he could avoid making a fool of himself again.

Clumsily he cleaned up in the bathroom. When he heard a key turn in the front door, he came out in time to see Natalie tote in two bags of groceries.

"You didn't have much food in the fridge," she said. "I figured I should get enough for a while."

"Bernie usually leaves a casserole on Saturdays," Patrick explained. "Otherwise, I pick up what I need from day to day." He never got around to planning his meals far enough in advance to do a week's shopping. "I'll reimburse you for that."

She handed him the receipt. "I hope you like spaghetti with clam sauce. Zucchini lasagna. Chicken and baked potatoes."

"You can cook all that?"

"I'm a woman of many talents," Natalie said.

There was a lot of food in those bags, Patrick noted as they went into the kitchen. And even more still in the car, he discovered when she fetched a second load. Almost too much, unless…

"Is what's-his-name going to be dining with us?" He tried to sound nonchalant.

"You don't mean my ex?"

"I assume since you've reconciled, you'd want him around." *Please say no,* he signaled her silently.

Natalie sputtered a couple of times before answering.

"No. I've decided that getting back together with Ralph was a mistake."

Relief loosened Patrick's grip on his crutch and nearly sent him sprawling. He eased into a chair. "Are you sure?"

"He's starting a business in Texas and I have no desire to move there." She transferred packages of meat and cheese into the refrigerator.

"That's the only problem?" Irrationally, he wanted her to declare that she found the man disgusting and had only gone to bed with him in a drunken stupor.

Natalie turned on the tap and rinsed her selection of fruits and vegetables. Patrick had to admit, he wasn't crazy about cauliflower, but he vowed to be a good sport this week. He'd eat anything she cooked, as long as he didn't have to put up with Ralph.

"He and I..." Natalie struggled to peel a sticker off an apple. "I wish they wouldn't put these labels on here. I hate it when I accidentally eat one."

Patrick was too impatient to wait for her to finish her original sentence. "It's over between you?"

"I wouldn't put it that way." Usually intuitive, Natalie was completely tuned out today. Patrick could have sworn she had no idea he was in an agony of suspense.

"How would you put it?"

"For the moment I'm letting the matter ride."

"Since you're having a baby together, I should think you'd need to come to some kind of agreement," he said. "Joint custody or whatever."

From a sack, Natalie removed a box of lasagna noodles and several boxes of spaghetti. "Let me worry about that."

As she walked to a cabinet, Patrick saw that her

abdomen had taken on an appealing curve. The baby, although still tiny, was growing.

The knowledge that it was Ralph's baby nagged at him. Not that he would hold it against the baby, which was an individual in its own right rather than a reflection of its parents. The problem was that, to Patrick's amazement, he envied the father.

An emotion welled up in him, more powerful than desire, more deep-seated than hunger. How would it feel to know Natalie was carrying his child? He pictured Kip and Kent playing in the pool, their faces bright with enthusiasm. To have a child of his own…

What on earth was he thinking?

"Are you falling asleep again?" Natalie asked. "If you are, let's get you to bed."

"I'm wide awake." Patrick glanced at his watch. Between the hospital and his nap, the afternoon had disappeared. "Let's start cooking. Show me what I can do to help." Although he rarely cooked anything complicated, he knew the basics.

"You can fix the salad," she said, and set the ingredients on the table where he could reach them.

AFTER DINNER they sat on the veranda at the back of the house. Accessible through French doors from the kitchen, living room and den, it overlooked the best view in Serene Beach.

From her comfortable, molded chair, Natalie could see the Pacific Coast highway unfurling below them and, beyond it, a panorama of coastline and harbor. Across the sky, pinks and yellows blazed against the lowering darkness.

She and Patrick were playing Go Fish. It was he who'd suggested the children's card game, saying his brain was too fuzzy to concentrate on anything more complicated.

Seated beside her, he studied his cards with pretend solemnity. "This is a great hand. I'm going to make fish bait out of you."

"Oh, yeah?" Natalie replied. "Well, I'm first. Got any tens?"

His eyebrows quirked mischievously. "Do I have to give you *all* my tens?"

"Every last one," she said, and took two. "Got any aces?"

"Go fish," he said gleefully.

They battled it out until Natalie won. Unfazed, Patrick won the second hand. She claimed the third and final victory.

"Beginner's luck," he said.

"I've been playing this game for years," she answered, tapping the deck into alignment and sliding it into its box.

"I meant, you're a beginner at my house," Patrick joked.

Although he didn't seem drugged anymore, he was more relaxed than she'd seen him in a long time. Natalie relished his company, yet if she'd realized he would be this much fun, she might not have dared agree to Bernie's request.

She found herself wanting to flirt with him. Instead, she blurted out the first neutral topic that came into her head. "Where do you suppose Heather's going on her leave?"

"You're the one with your ear to the ground," Patrick said. "What's the prevailing theory among the staff?"

"Nothing but wild guesses," Natalie said. "Why

would she suddenly decide she needed two months' leave?''

"Maybe she's a secret operative for the CIA." Patrick leaned forward, enjoying the new game. "Heading to a war-torn country on a mission."

"To deliver the sultan's heir," Natalie said, joining the game.

"The sultan could afford his own doctor," Patrick pointed out. "No, she's delivering the secret baby of...of..."

"A peasant woman."

"And this birth is important because...?"

"There's a prophecy!" she invented. "On this baby rests the fate of the nation."

"When he grows up, he'll—"

"She," she corrected. "When she grows up, she'll bring the people together by..."

"...recording a new version of..."

"'Bridge Over Troubled Water!'" Natalie said.

Patrick shook his head. "'Yellow Polka Dot Bikini,'" he said.

She chuckled and stretched her legs beneath the table. "You must love sitting out here in the evenings. It's beautiful."

"When my parents built this house, my dad swore he was going to barbecue out here," Patrick said. "He never even got around to buying a grill."

"Why not?"

His mouth tightened. "He never took the pressure off himself long enough."

"Sounds like someone else I know," Natalie said.

"That's why I'm not going to repeat my father's mistakes," Patrick said. "He had kids and then was hardly ever around. Thanks to my mom, Bernie and I had a wonderful childhood, but there's no substitute for a father. I would never raise a child that way.''

''And you don't think you mattered to him?'' she asked.

''He hardly even noticed we were here.''

''Maybe he noticed more than you think,'' she said. ''Surely he knew his family was here for him, even when he was working his hardest. Otherwise he'd have been awfully lonely, don't you think?''

The fading sunset reflected in Patrick's eyes, giving them an unaccustomed opaqueness. ''If you work hard enough, you don't have time to be lonely.''

''If you work hard enough, you don't have time to live, either,'' she said, saddened that he hadn't come to the realization that his father had needed others and that he did, too.

''I guess I'll find out.''

As they lapsed into silence, Natalie became aware of how close they were. His arm rested on the edge of his chair, inches from her side, and his long legs nearly brushed hers. In the cool air, warmth radiated from his skin to hers.

''I'm concerned about how you're going to manage a baby by yourself.'' Patrick shifted to look directly at her. An electric current sizzled between them.

''My mother will help.'' Deliberately, Natalie closed her eyes to break the connection.

''Who's going to be your labor coach?'' he asked.

''I don't know. Maybe I'll ask Amy.''

''After the baby's born, you'll need someone you can call at any hour if he gets sick or you're exhausted and need relief,'' Patrick went on. ''Your mom's got a life of her own.''

Natalie sighed. "Other single moms muddle through, and I will, too."

"You shouldn't have to," he said more to himself than to her.

"Are you suggesting I ask Ralph to move in with me?" Natalie asked.

His response was instantaneous and gratifying: an expression of dismay, followed by a fruitless attempt to disguise his reaction. With considerable tact, considering how much he obviously disliked Ralph, he said, "He doesn't strike me as the kind of man you can rely on."

"You're right," she said.

"In that case, I don't understand why you decided to get involved with him again."

It was impossible to respond without telling more lies. Besides, even Natalie's active imagination couldn't summon a reason for reconciling with Ralph.

"You need your beauty sleep, Dr. Barr," she said.

"You're changing the subject."

"Darn right." She stood up. "Can I give you a hand?"

"I'm not entirely helpless," Patrick said.

"Suit yourself." She let him struggle to his feet. His muscles would be extra sore tomorrow because of his stubbornness, but that was his choice.

"There's one slight problem," Patrick said as they crossed the den. "My pajamas and toothbrush are upstairs."

"I'll get them."

"Thanks."

Natalie made her way to the curving staircase. Halfway up, she couldn't resist stopping to look over the elegant foyer.

Play the Romance Crossword Game

and get...
2 FREE BOOKS
and a
FREE GIFT...
YOURS to KEEP!

Scratch Here!

to reveal the hidden words.
Look below to see what you get.

Yes!

I have scratched off the gold areas. Please send me my **2 FREE BOOKS** and **FREE GIFT** for which I qualify. I understand that I am under no obligation to purchase any books as explained on the back of this card.

▶ **DETACH AND MAIL CARD TODAY!** ▶

354 HDL DRTY   154 HDL DRUG

FIRST NAME   LAST NAME

ADDRESS

APT.#   CITY

STATE/PROV.   ZIP/POSTAL CODE

Visit us online at
www.eHarlequin.com

ROMANCE	MYSTERY	NOVEL	GIFT
You get **2 FREE BOOKS** PLUS a **FREE GIFT!**	You get **2 FREE BOOKS!**	You get **1 FREE BOOK!**	You get a **FREE MYSTERY GIFT!**

The Harlequin Reader Service® — Here's how it works:

Accepting your 2 free books and mystery gift places you under no obligation to buy anything. You may keep the books and gift and return the shipping statement marked "cancel." If you do not cancel, about a month later we'll send you 4 additional books and bill you just $3.99 each in the U.S., or $4.74 each in Canada, plus 25¢ shipping & handling per book and applicable taxes if any.* That's the complete price and — compared to cover prices of $4.75 each in the U.S. and $5.75 each in Canada — it's quite a bargain! You may cancel at any time, but if you choose to continue, every month we'll send you 4 more books, which you may either purchase at the discount price or return to us and cancel your subscription.

*Terms and prices subject to change without notice. Sales tax applicable in N.Y. Canadian residents will be charged applicable provincial taxes and GST. Credit or Debit balances in a customer's account(s) may be offset by any other outstanding balance owed by or to the customer

She imagined how exciting it must have been for Bernie years ago, sweeping down these steps in her stunning cherry-red prom dress. Her parents' faces must have shone with pride as they watched.

Natalie knew about the dress because later it had been among a group of designer dresses raffled off to raise money for the Doctors Circle, which was only in the planning stage. Natalie had bought two tickets and dreamed, in vain, of winning one for her own prom.

Instead, she'd worn a made-over dress of Candy's. When her date arrived, Natalie had hurried outside to meet him so he wouldn't see her mother's boyfriend of the time watching TV in the living room, his sleeveless T-shirt riding high on his beer belly.

She and the Barrs had grown up very differently, Natalie mused as she continued on her way. Yet, in a sense, all of them had missed having a father.

Although she'd visited the house a number of times, she'd never ventured onto the second floor. When she reached the landing, she saw that the area around the top of the stairs had been left open to form a lounge.

On one side, toward the front of the house, there was only a high, round window above a wet bar. On the other, however, glass doors flanked by padded benches opened onto a balcony. A person could sit here and read within sight and sound of the Pacific.

A home like this was almost too splendid for real people to live in. Natalie took a deep breath and went to look for Patrick's room.

The first two bedchambers she peeked into were well appointed but clearly unoccupied. The master suite was another story, humming with electronic equipment and lightly scented with the lime of Patrick's cologne.

The desk sported a computer, even though there was

also one downstairs in his office. An entertainment center faced the king-size waterbed, where a pillow bore the indentation of his head.

Reminding herself of the reason she'd come, Natalie opened a drawer in the bureau to look for pajamas. Finding only neatly folded male underwear, she closed it swiftly and checked below. Only a folded blanket and an extra pillow.

Next stop, the walk-in closet. Nearly as large as Natalie's living room, it came with sliding racks that reminded her of a dry-cleaning establishment. There were an amazing number of suits, shirts, slacks, belts, ties and shoes, each of which had passed through Patrick's hands and been worn on his body. She shivered involuntarily, as if he'd touched her without warning.

Spotting a pair of blue pajamas traced with gray stripes, Natalie snatched them and exited the closet. Embarrassed by her reaction to what was, after all, simply a bedchamber, she went into the bathroom.

Gleaming blue tile meandered between a whirlpool bath, a shower stall and twin sinks. Natalie collected Patrick's toothbrush and toothpaste, brush, comb and shaving gear.

She went downstairs and laid the items on his bed in the office. He was sitting at the desk, checking the hospital's website.

"Loretta did a fine job of posting Dr. Carmichael's photo and the press release," he said. "She seemed very excited about his coming here, didn't she?"

"She's trying to get pregnant," Natalie said without thinking. "Oh, dear. I shouldn't have mentioned that."

"I hope Dr. Carmichael can help her," Patrick said. "I'm sorry, I've been so distracted lately that I haven't asked how you're doing. Any stomach upsets or other problems?''

''Nothing serious.'' Natalie's initial nausea had recurred a couple of times, but hadn't settled into daylong misery as it did with some women. ''I do get tired easily. Right now I'm ready to collapse.'' She hadn't known that until she spoke the words, but now the weariness washed over her.

''Go make yourself at home. Sleep wherever you like,'' Patrick said.

''I'll make up one of the spare beds. Or maybe they're ready, like the couch was,'' she said.

''I'm not sure. The housekeeper takes care of that.'' He started to get up, and flinched. ''I keep forgetting about my ankle.''

''Need help getting into bed?'' Natalie asked.

''Let's not push our luck.''

So he, too, felt this temptation to throw common sense out the window. In spite of his injury and in spite of what they both knew was best, they skated near the brink of doing exactly what they'd done on the yacht.

''I'd better go.'' She backed away.

''See you in the morning.''

Natalie fled. She wanted so much to hold him that it was like a physical ache. The more distance she put between them, the better.

Upstairs, hauling her suitcase, she discovered that neither of the smaller beds was fitted with sheets. Although there had to be a linen closet somewhere, a quick search failed to find it. Maybe it was downstairs in the laundry room off the kitchen.

Natalie's muscles were turning to rubber, and a sandy sleepiness threatened to deposit her right on the carpet. Reluctantly she made her way into the master bedroom.

It was so full of Patrick's presence that he might as well have still been here. No, that wasn't true. She was perfectly safe up here, from him and from herself.

She set the suitcase on a small table and took out her nightgown, which for caution's sake was a long flannel one she'd found in the back of her closet. Barely summoning the strength to change and brush her teeth, she sank into bed, her head against the pillow where last night Patrick's had been.

Bathed in his essence, she fell asleep.

ON SUNDAY a steady string of people came to call, offering food and best wishes for Patrick's recovery. As a result, Natalie didn't have to worry about being alone with him.

A lot of people had learned of the injury thanks to a reporter for the local newspaper, who'd written a dramatic account of Patrick's rescuing his sister from a watery grave. Among the visitors were not only staff members at Doctors Circle but patrons and friends from the yacht club.

Noreen McLanahan arrived in the afternoon, bearing a box of chocolate bunnies. "These are for you," she told Natalie. "You're the real hero, moving in here to take care of your boss."

"Thanks. Bernie twisted my arm," she confided, accepting the gift. "Go on into the living room. Patrick's holding court."

"I'll take a peek." The older woman walked quietly across the foyer and peered into the vast, sunken room where Patrick occupied one couch, his leg elevated. He was talking with the mayor and the president of a medical-implements manufacturing firm.

"The usual rich old fogies," Noreen whispered, although she was older than either of the two men and just as wealthy. "I hope Patrick's hitting them up for big donations to the Endowment Fund, but frankly, they bore me to tears."

"How about coffee in the kitchen?"

"Sounds great."

Over cups of decaf, the two of them discussed the latest comings and goings at Doctors Circle. Every time they were interrupted by the doorbell, Natalie escorted the new arrivals into the living room and returned.

Bernie came bustling in with her family in tow. Loretta arrived with her sister, Rita, and they were followed minutes later by Finn Sorrell.

"Playing hostess, I see," the police chief said to Natalie. "Don't get too comfortable, Mrs. Winford. Men like Patrick Barr may amuse themselves with someone like you, but it doesn't last long."

"You suffer from an overactive imagination," Natalie answered tartly. "I'm assisting Dr. Barr at the request of his sister. If you don't believe me, ask her. And it's been *Ms.* Winford for nearly six years. Perhaps you should have your memory tested."

She stalked back to the kitchen. "You've got steam coming out of your ears," Noreen said.

"That was Finn Sorrell," she explained.

"He and his brother blow so much hot air the county fair ought to give them the balloon concession." Noreen huffed. "Sit down and let's discuss something more pleasant, like your mother's wonderful dolls. I just bought one at the gift shop."

A short time later Loretta and Rita slipped into the

kitchen. "Oh, good, we were looking for you," the PR director told Natalie. "And it's delightful to see you, Mrs. McLanahan."

"No wonder you folks are hiding in here," Rita said. "Chief Sorrell is such a blowhard!"

Her sister frowned. "You shouldn't talk about community leaders that way. It's my job to win over people like him."

"And he buys his cars at my husband's dealership, so he's a valued customer. That doesn't mean I have to get chummy with him." Waving away her sister's offer to fill a mug for her, Rita looked around. "Do you have any tea? Coffee disagrees with me these days."

As Natalie fetched some from a cabinet, Noreen said, "Don't tell me we've got two expectant mothers here. I hear some women stop liking coffee the minute those hormones hit the bloodstream."

Rita opened her mouth, but no words came out. Seeing her sister's reaction, Loretta went white.

"Uh-oh," Natalie said.

Noreen peered from one sister to the other. "Something tells me I just put my foot in my mouth. There's no fool like an old fool."

"You had no way of knowing it was a ticklish situation," Rita said. "Loretta, I should have told you sooner. I kept hoping you'd get pregnant, too, and then you wouldn't be so disheartened."

Recovering, Loretta bristled at her. "Do you think I'd resent having a niece or nephew? Sis, I'm thrilled for you."

"But it has to hurt," Rita said. "I know how much you want a baby."

"Now that Dr. Carmichael's coming, I've got new

hope. I do wish Dr. Rourke wasn't leaving right now, though.'' Loretta's mug trembled slightly. Natalie's heart went out to her.

''Yes, what's going on with Dr. Rourke?'' Noreen said.

She'd neatly changed the topic, but as the women chewed over possible reasons for Heather's taking leave, Loretta's tension remained evident.

Natalie hoped Dr. Carmichael could work the miracle Loretta hoped for. That was what Doctors Circle was all about, after all.

By dinnertime, everyone had left except for Bernie's family. Her husband sent out for Chinese food, to his sons' delight.

They ate on the veranda. Natalie, who had discovered fresh linens stored beneath the built-in seats in the upstairs lounge, excused herself early and went to the spare bedroom to which she'd transferred her belongings.

For one evening at least, she'd avoided being alone with Patrick. Having people around made it easier to resist her impulse to touch him and invite intimacies that could only lead to trouble. But since his ankle hurt him as much today as yesterday, she knew she had to hold out for a few more days before she could go home.

She wasn't sure it was possible.

Chapter Ten

On Monday, when the housekeeper arrived, Natalie departed for the office to catch up on mail and phone messages. Although Patrick knew the work needed to be done, he found himself looking up whenever a floorboard creaked and feeling disappointed when she failed to appear.

Not that he wasn't busy himself. The latest weather report called for a chance of rain on Saturday, so he ordered tents erected for the band and caterer. He devoted most of the morning to polishing his brief speech for the event.

The Oktoberfest loomed large in the future of the Endowment Fund. The yacht party had brought in a respectable two million dollars, but it fell far short of the thirty million needed, with only seven months to go.

Patrick knew the press would trumpet the fact if he and the center came nowhere near their goal. It might even hurt future fund-raising efforts. Had he been recklessly optimistic? Should he have scheduled more time than the symbolic nine months he'd allotted for the campaign?

He simply had to prevail. If that meant working

while his ankle throbbed, it was a small price to pay to ensure the future of Doctors Circle. He only hoped one of the well-to-do guests, particularly a videogame company owner that Loretta had been cultivating, would decide to become a major supporter.

Outside, he heard a vehicle rattle up the driveway. Through the blinds, Patrick watched a rusty pickup truck with Texas license plates halt in the parking bay. He'd never seen the vehicle before, but he had a pretty good idea whose it was.

Natalie hadn't returned from the office yet. In her absence, Patrick decided it was his duty to get rid of her ex-husband.

For her sake. For his sake. For the sake of a poor little kid who deserved a decent father, although where such a man was to be found, Patrick hadn't figured out yet.

He grabbed his crutch and swung out of the room just as the doorbell chimed. Mrs. Frick, the housekeeper, started to answer but Patrick politely waved her away. When he opened the door, there—as expected— stood Ralph, a cowboy hat perched atop his sparse red hair.

"What can I do for you?" Patrick asked.

"Howdy, Dr. Barr." The fellow gave him a toothy grin. Obviously he was doing his best to go native since moving to Texas, probably to the annoyance of the real Texans. "I hear my Natalie's playing Florence Nightingale. How's she getting along?"

"She's fine. Was she expecting you?" He blocked the doorway and pretended not to notice as the visitor tried to edge inside.

"Not exactly, but what's the difference?" Ralph said. "I've got a hankering to speak to my wife."

"Your wife? Does this mean you're still married?" It was a challenge, not question.

"You know how it goes." The man's smug tone of voice grated on Patrick's nerves. "One piece of paper doesn't make much difference."

"Are you referring to your divorce papers or your marriage license?" Patrick asked.

"I don't see how it's your concern." The creases on Ralph's forehead deepened. "Wait a minute. Her mother said you'd been hurt bad, but you don't look so helpless to me. I'm starting to think there's some hanky-panky going on here."

As if his relationship with Natalie was this jerk's business! Patrick felt an urge to hoist the guy over his head and fling him across the driveway. Right, and whose leg was he going to stand on while he did it?

"She'll be back any minute," he said tautly. "Until I learn whether or not she wants to talk to you, you can wait in your truck."

About to close the door, he caught a flash of green coming up the driveway. Ralph must have heard Natalie's car, too, because he turned, then swung back with a look of triumph. "I guess I'm about to have a chat with her, after all, Doc. You might want to put a lid on that jealousy of yours."

Patrick chose not to dignify the remark with a retort. Instead, he propped himself in the doorway and waited.

Natalie parked and got out. There was no hint of welcome on her face when she spotted her ex-husband. "Well?" she demanded.

"Honey…" He glanced at Patrick. "Do you mind? This is a personal conversation."

"Be my guest." Leaving the door unlocked, Patrick

retreated to his study. Despite his curiosity, he respected Natalie's privacy.

Inside, he could hear raised voices through the open window. He went to close it, but had to struggle to navigate the obstacle course of furniture.

"I'm glad your buddies want to be partners in the garage," Natalie was saying. "I wasn't going to lend you the money in any case."

"Forget the money. How about taking one more chance on me? We had a good thing going, kid."

"Good for whom?" she snapped.

Patrick would have liked to hear more, but he finally got his hands on the sash, and to listen further would be eavesdropping. Reluctantly he blocked out the rest of their words.

Ralph was utterly wrong for Natalie. Why had he come back into the picture? Why on earth had she slept with the man again?

Ralph must have manipulated her. He'd doubtless known, which Patrick hadn't, that Natalie longed for a child. Subconsciously, that must have made her vulnerable.

Why couldn't she be having a child with me, instead?

Patrick froze. Surely he didn't mean that. It was the most selfish idea he'd ever had.

He wanted Natalie to find happiness. And that was one thing he couldn't offer her.

Mrs. Frick tapped on the office door, which he'd left ajar. "I can fix your lunch now if you'd like, Dr. Barr."

"No, thanks. Go ahead and take your break," he said.

"It's such a lovely day, I'm planning to eat on the

veranda.'' Sympathetically, the gray-haired house-keeper indicated his ankle. ''You're sure I can't fix you anything?''

''Enjoy your lunch.'' He barely refrained from telling her to take the afternoon off so he could be alone with Natalie. Mrs. Frick adhered to a self-imposed schedule of tasks, and sending her home early would upset her.

It was a relief when he heard the truck clatter away down the driveway. Patrick waited, trying to read over his speech and unable to focus on a single word.

In the foyer Natalie's footsteps clicked across the floor, back and forth. Although Patrick told himself to pay no attention, he could hear her muttering—no clear words, just an outraged buzz.

A while later she came into his office, her blue eyes sparkling with angry tears. ''I'm sorry that man inflicted himself on you.''

Patrick forced himself not to exult in Ralph's defeat. He had no right to meddle in his secretary's affairs, especially considering that she was bearing this man's child. ''I hope things are working out the way you want.''

''He's going back to Texas,'' Natalie said. ''He figured he could hit me up for the money to start his own garage. I'm glad he found some friends to go in with him and I wish him luck, as long as he stays far away from me.''

''You should talk to a lawyer,'' Patrick said.

''Why?''

''Child support.'' Maybe it was none of his business, but someone had to look out for Natalie's interests.

''Trying to get money out of Ralph would be about

as productive as asking a turtle to sing," she said. "It's not in his nature."

"I'm glad he's gone," Patrick admitted. "You don't need a leech like that."

She regarded him with an unreadable expression. "What kind of man do I need?"

"The kind of man I wish I were." He meant it, deeply.

Natalie smoothed down her blouse, apparently unaware of how sexy the movement looked. "What would you do if you were in Ralph's position? What if you'd gotten your ex-wife or your girlfriend pregnant and the two of you couldn't work things out?"

"I'd insist on counseling," Patrick said. "If that failed, I'd do what's best for her. Even if it meant giving her up to a better man."

"If she could find a better man," Natalie said wistfully.

"I've often wondered what would have happened if my mother had left Dad. She nearly did, once, when Bernie and I were teenagers." Patrick had never shared his family secrets with anyone except his sister, but he wanted Natalie to understand his parents, because it might help her understand him. "Maybe she'd have met someone who took the time to make her happy."

"That surprises me," she said. "I only met your father a few times, but I got to know your mom later on. I don't think she could have loved anyone else as much as she loved him. Not to mention the way you and your sister doted on him."

Patrick leaned back in the desk chair and flexed his leg to keep it from stiffening. "Bernie and I adored him, but we were never really close. I don't think it ever occurred to him to read to us or take us to the beach.''

''At least he stuck around. My father left when I was ten,'' Natalie said.

''I'm sorry.'' Patrick couldn't imagine a childhood without the firm foundation of a father, even a remote one. ''It must have been hard on your mother, too.''

Blond hair tumbled across one cheek as Natalie stared down at her lap. ''Angie got married three times and had boyfriends in between. When one relationship failed, she always rebounded. But your mother was different. What made her think of leaving?''

''She was terribly unhappy after we moved here,'' he said. ''She and Dad had built this big house, and she'd expected them to spend time together swimming, barbecuing, doing things like that.''

''Angie had this cranky barbecue that sometimes burst into flames and charred the chicken,'' Natalie said. ''She used to tell her boyfriends to go out in back of the trailer and make a burnt offering.''

Patrick wished his mother had known Angie. With her spunk and sense of humor, she'd have been a good influence. ''Mom felt isolated and lonely in this big house. Dad was working night and day on plans for Doctors Circle, and Bernie was going through her I'm-thirteen-and-I-hate-the-world phase.''

''Whereas you were the perfect child?'' Natalie teased.

''I was seventeen and in love with the car my parents gave me for getting straight A's,'' he admitted. ''The only time I listened to Mom's problems was when I insisted on chauffeuring her places to have an excuse to drive.''

''At least you listened,'' she said.

"One time she mentioned that we might all be better off if she and Dad split up. That way, at least he'd spend the occasional weekend with Bernie and me," Patrick said. "I was so shocked when she said that, I almost lost control of the car."

"What did you say?"

"I told her it wouldn't help unless he also spent some of his weekends with her." Later he'd realized the advice, although self-serving because he didn't want his parents to split up, had probably been what his mother needed to hear. "A few days afterward, she told me that she'd decided it would hurt too many people if she left and that she'd be even lonelier."

"That's a sad story," Natalie said.

"Not entirely." Although Patrick wished his parents had entered counseling, he knew Joe wouldn't have considered it. "She threw herself into working on Doctors Circle, too. They spent more time together that way, and she seemed happier."

"What about your father? Was he happier?"

"He was like me," Patrick said. "To him, pursuing his own happiness would have meant being selfish. He couldn't rest unless he was doing his duty."

"He had a duty to his wife and kids," Natalie pointed out.

"You said earlier that certain things aren't in Ralph's nature," Patrick said. "I'm afraid certain things aren't in my nature, either."

"I thought we were talking about your parents."

"I meant my dad's and mine," Patrick said. "We're a lot alike."

She considered this statement before responding. "You're driven, I agree. After watching you with your nephews, though, I don't think you're giving yourself enough credit. You'd make a good family man.''

The observation settled into Patrick's mind like a speck of dust, too minor to notice, yet too irritating to ignore. He found himself musing on it during lunch and that afternoon while Natalie reviewed applications for the secretarial position. It troubled him so much he began to wonder if he ought to reexamine his assumptions.

Maybe he wasn't exactly like his father. The question remained: How different was he?

AFTER DINNER, as they walked to the den to watch TV, Natalie said, ''You're moving as if your muscles are tightening up.'' Watching him made her feel a bit stiff herself, a sort of instinctive sympathy.

Patrick lurched a little on his crutch. ''Maybe I should arrange for a massage.''

''You mean have one of the nurses come over?'' she said.

''The yacht club employs a masseuse,'' Patrick explained. ''She's available to visit members at home if they're ill or injured.''

In the den Natalie watched him lower himself onto the couch. Since the housekeeper departed, she'd felt almost as if she and Patrick were a couple, staying home together. Even his preoccupied air during dinner had been comfortable. Only people who knew each other well didn't feel obliged to search for topics of conversation.

Now, the prospect of having a strange woman put her hands all over Patrick irked Natalie. For heaven's sake, she knew how to give a massage, too!

''I could do it,'' she said.

"Do what?" Patrick clicked on a baseball game.

"Give you a massage." Spoken aloud, the proposal sounded brazen, so she added, "I took a class in therapeutic massage after my mother broke her leg."

"You don't have one of those portable tables. You'd hurt your back bending over me," he said.

"I can manage."

He clicked off the game and regarded Natalie thoughtfully. "Are you sure that's a good idea? The two of us alone in the house... I realize we've gotten past all that, but why tempt fate?"

"Don't worry," she said. "There won't be anything personal about it."

"I can't take advantage of you that way." Patrick picked up the phone and rapid-dialed, listened to a recording and then punched in a number. After a moment he hung up. "She's gone for the day."

"So much for your massage." Natalie had no intention of offering again. "Too bad you turned me down while you had the chance."

"You're a vindictive woman," he teased, and turned the TV set back on. Loud static made them both jump. The screen flickered with black-and-white ghosts. "Darn cable. That's the second time it's gone out this month."

"You should get satellite."

"There's a shelf of videos..." He shook his head and turned off the TV. "Forget it. The options are crawling up the stairs so I can use the whirlpool, which I don't think I'm quite up to doing yet, or going to bed and suffering."

"You could use a dose of suffering." Natalie folded her arms. "It might make you more appreciative in the future when somebody makes you a generous offer."

He cast her a look of puppy-dog hurt. "You'd really abandon me? I was only trying to spare your back."

"Oh, all right." She hadn't intended to hold out for long, anyway. "Lie down and tell me where it hurts."

"Arms, shoulders, back, legs," Patrick said promptly.

"In other words, everywhere."

"That about covers it."

She decided it was safest if he left his clothing on, even though she couldn't give him a thorough rub that way. "Just stretch out, then."

Patrick obeyed, although his long legs and strong build made him almost too large for the couch. Natalie perched on the edge.

The moment her fingers made contact, guilty pleasure rippled through her. *We've gotten past all that.* Not even a little bit!

Determined to do the job as promised, she began working on his lower back. Beneath her firm hand pressure, she could feel the muscles resisting, then slowly yielding.

She steadily worked her way up Patrick's spine and along the shoulder blades, thrusting gently to overcome the tautness. A low moan of satisfaction rolled from him.

She moved down again, to his lower back and across his tight, muscular buttocks to the corded strength of his thighs. Everywhere, the tension eased beneath her probing hands, yet she detected a kind of pleasant readiness. A hum of anticipation.

Awareness of him tingled in Natalie's lips, in the tips of her breasts, in her sensual core. She imagined herself kissing the nape of his neck, imagined him rolling over, his hands reaching for her...

She stopped massaging abruptly. "That's enough for now."

"We were just getting started." His voice sounded hoarse.

"You're right about the couch. It's too low." She stood up. "You should call the masseuse tomorrow."

Patrick eased himself into a sitting position. Mussed brown hair fell rakishly across his forehead as he studied her. "That was great. I wish it could've lasted forever."

If she sat down, right where she'd been a moment ago, he could easily draw her into his arms. And he would, Natalie knew. Even though he believed she was pregnant with Ralph's baby, that wouldn't stop him from making love to her.

The connection between them was so strong she almost didn't want to fight it. So strong, and such a threat to her happiness, because of her own lies and his commitment to high standards. They would combust, first in ecstasy and later with recrimination.

Natalie knew how many ways love could go wrong. It had happened to her marriage, and she'd seen it many times in her mother's life. Sometimes the joy might be worth it, but she'd already had her night of craziness with Patrick. Twice in one lifetime was too much to ask.

She changed the subject. "At lunchtime tomorrow I'm interviewing three women for the job of Dr. Carmichael's secretary." She didn't mention, because it was so personal, that she also planned to keep an appointment with Heather. Natalie had been grateful to squeeze in one more checkup before her friend's departure.

"I'm glad you're moving ahead aggressively," Patrick said. "Jason wants her to start in January, which isn't as far off as it seems."

"I suppose not," Natalie said. "I hope you don't mind my leaving you alone for an hour or so."

Patrick raised his eyebrows mockingly. "Bernie will be scandalized."

"I'm only going across the street," Natalie reminded him unnecessarily. "You know, that would be a good time to schedule your massage."

"Great idea." The playfulness ebbed as Patrick got to his feet. "Thanks for the back rub. It made me loose enough to skip the painkiller tonight, and that means a clearer head tomorrow."

"You'll need it," Natalie said.

Loretta was coming over in the afternoon to review strategies for the Oktoberfest. Several corporate leaders needed to be wooed with a deft touch, especially Alfred LoBianco, whose company was introducing a hot new videogame that could rake in millions.

He was reputed to be seeking a charitable project to adopt. By coincidence, his company, WiseWorld Global Productions, had a circular logo similar to the one used by the center. In addition, it already sponsored several youth-oriented programs. The two were a natural fit.

"Good night, then." Patrick's gaze lingered on hers. "Sleep well."

He hesitated. Natalie knew him well enough to see that something was bothering him. In this case it might be better if she didn't probe into the matter.

With a faint smile, she hurried upstairs. At the top she listened to his shuffling movements until the office door closed.

He'd made it to his room in one piece. And she'd escaped the temptation to indulge in utter folly.

Or perhaps in never-to-be-recaptured bliss.

Chapter Eleven

When she heard her name called at Heather's office, Natalie noticed at once that Cynthia was wearing maternity clothes. The dark-haired nurse looked, if anything, more troubled than ever.

It didn't take a mind reader to guess that Cynthia's married boyfriend wasn't standing by her. "Is there anything I can do to help?" Natalie asked as she stepped onto the scale.

"What?" Cynthia regarded her in surprise. "Oh, you mean this." She indicated her smock embroidered with a baby motif. "I guess we're in the same boat, aren't we."

"It looks that way," Natalie said. "When are you due?"

"May fifteenth." Catching Natalie's dubious expression, the nurse said, "I know I'm getting big fast. I had an ultrasound—it's twins."

"Congratulations."

"Thanks, I guess."

They went into the examining room. "You know, Dr. Barr set up a fund to help employees in difficulty," Natalie said while Cynthia was taking her blood pressure. "I'll bring you an application form if you're interested."

"I don't need any help right now, but thanks," the nurse answered. "I do wish Dr. Rourke wasn't leaving, though."

"She'll be back in plenty of time for our deliveries," Natalie said. "I assume you'll be assisting the new doctor while she's gone."

Cynthia made a wry face. "I'm glad it's only for two months. In my present mood, I prefer having a woman boss."

After she left, Heather came in. The red-haired obstetrician bubbled with excitement. "If you had anything to do with Patrick's granting my leave, thank you."

"You don't have to act so happy about going away!" Natalie admonished teasingly.

"I'll miss my patients, and I don't mean to let people down." The doctor listened to Natalie's heartbeat and double-checked her blood pressure, even though Cynthia had just taken it. "I suppose I'm being selfish."

"It's not so bad for me," Natalie said. "Loretta's so anxious to get pregnant that it might be more of a problem for her."

"I don't usually discuss patients, but since you bring it up, I am concerned about her," Heather said. "She seems very tense. Anxiety can make it even harder to conceive."

"She found out that Rita's having a baby," Natalie said.

Heather sighed. "It's a touchy situation. I wish I could persuade her to talk to Amy. Counselors can help infertility patients come to terms with their situation.

We can't all have babies, and then, of course, sometimes we have them when we don't plan to.''

"Don't worry about me," Natalie said. "I'll work it
out.''

"Oh! I didn't mean you. I was talking about myself.'' Heather took a deep breath. "I've got to tell
someone or I'll burst.'' She checked her watch.
"You're my last patient before lunch. Do you have a
minute?''

"You bet.'' Half an hour remained before the first
secretarial candidate was to arrive.

After Heather pronounced Natalie in great shape,
they adjourned to her small, book-crammed office
down the hall. Next May, in the remodeled wing, she'd
have at least twice the space.

They poured themselves cups of coffee and settled
onto two upholstered chairs. "This is a secret from
absolutely everyone except Amy," Heather said.

"I promise.'' Natalie could hardly breathe. "What's
going on?''

"I haven't told anybody all these years.'' Absent-
mindedly, the small, intense woman twisted an auburn
curl around her finger. "My sophomore year in high
school, I got pregnant. When my boyfriend found out,
he wanted nothing to do with me, and I gave up our
daughter for adoption.''

Natalie understood now why Heather had suggested
that adoption wasn't such a bad idea. "It turned out all
right for you?''

"It was hard sometimes, knowing I had a child
somewhere growing up without me.'' Her eyes got a
faraway look. "I worried and wondered about her. But
I knew it was for the best. She'd gone to two loving
parents and I was able to get on with my life. Maybe

not perfectly, since I've had a hard time trusting men, but I can't complain.''

''What's changed?'' Natalie asked.

''A few months ago, she e-mailed me. I'd put my name into an Internet registry, in case she ever needed to contact me for medical reasons,'' Heather said.

''Is she all right?''

''She's fine. Unfortunately her adoptive parents were killed in a plane crash last year, but she's almost twenty-one and they left her enough money to finish college.''

''Did you meet her?'' Natalie said.

''Last month I drove to Los Angeles and we had lunch.'' Heather smiled dreamily. ''Olive's a delightful person, very articulate and creative. She was fascinated to learn that I'm an obstetrician. Here's the amazing part—she's pregnant. That's why she wanted to meet me and learn about her genetic heritage.''

''You're going to be a grandmother? No wonder you're excited!'' Natalie said. ''When's she due?''

''In about two weeks.''

So that was why the doctor wanted leave! ''She asked you to be there?''

''Her fiancé is in the Marines, and he's being sent overseas,'' Heather explained. ''When she found out, she called me in a panic. She doesn't have any other family and she wants me to coach her when she gives birth and to stay with her afterward, to help with the baby. How could I say no?''

''No way on earth.'' Natalie was thrilled for her friend. ''You're not going to handle the delivery yourself, are you?''

''I'm too emotionally involved,'' Heather said. ''Besides, she doesn't need me there as a doctor—she needs me to be her mom. That's what she said! I realize I'm not the mother who raised her, the one she'd prefer to have with her, but I'm the next best thing.''

''I think it's wonderful that you can help her this way,'' Natalie said. ''It'll give you a chance to bond with your grandchild, too.''

At thirty-six, Heather looked about as far from grandmotherly as Natalie could imagine, but her eyes were shining. ''That's right. Isn't it incredible?''

''You may find it hard not to brag about your beautiful grandchild when you get home,'' Natalie warned.

''I'll show you and Amy the pictures,'' Heather promised. ''As for everyone else, well, I know most people these days accept out-of-wedlock births, but I don't want my private life to become public gossip.''

''I won't tell anyone.'' Natalie understood what it was like to have embarrassing secrets. ''Please e-mail me while you're away and let me know how things are going.''

''Of course,'' Heather said.

''And give Olive my best regards. I hope I get to meet her someday.''

The two parted warmly. Natalie was grateful that her friend had shared this confidence, and glad to know there was such an upbeat reason for her leavetaking.

On the way to the administration building, she bought a tuna sandwich at the coffee kiosk, then ate it upstairs in the nearly empty lunchroom. Despite the refrigerator and microwave oven, most employees preferred to eat outdoors or walk across the courtyard to the cafeteria in the Birthing Center.

To Natalie, this room, like this building and the entire complex, was her home. At the center of it, she conceded silently, stood Patrick.

She relived the experience of touching him last night. His tantalizing masculine scent came back to her, along with the feel of his firm body beneath her palms.

What she experienced when she was with him went beyond friendship or even sex. It was a supreme sense of rightness and belonging.

At the same time, she knew she didn't really belong with him. Her chaotic upbringing, her disastrous marriage, the lies on her job application—they were like stones piled so high they formed a barrier.

Guiltily Natalie reflected that she'd made matters worse by allowing him to believe that Ralph was the father of her child. It was wrong, yet the deception helped preserve everything that mattered to her, including Patrick's trust.

His trust. Oh, how misplaced that was!

Once again she'd taken the easy way out. She'd talked herself into lying—by inaction, true, but she'd still perpetrated a falsehood—rather than face the consequences of her own actions. Natalie didn't see any way out of this maze that wouldn't result in utter disaster.

She heard the elevator doors open and realized it was time for her first appointment. Downing the last bite of sandwich, Natalie went out to greet the first secretarial candidate.

A generously built woman in her forties, Nan Ryerson had been working for a temporary secretarial agency ever since her divorce. Although Natalie liked her, she seemed too chatty and motherly to suit Dr. Carmichael. She'd be perfect for a receptionist position, however, and Natalie made a note to that effect.

The second applicant was a polite, well-groomed young woman named Coral Liu. In her late twenties, she seemed a bit low-key to handle the fiery Dr. Carmichael, but she had a steady manner and excellent qualifications. Natalie decided to keep her in mind for the position.

The last of the day's interviewees, Ruth Snippett, had maroon hair and a take-charge manner. Laid off during cutbacks at a Los Angeles hospital, she was in her midthirties and clearly ready to get on with a new job.

She was about to go to the head of the list when the woman asked about Natalie's own salary and position. ''I heard via the grapevine that you're having a baby. I figure the director will need to replace you in a few months, so I'd like to be considered for that job, too.''

''I'll only be gone a short time,'' she said. ''This interview is for the job of Dr. Carmichael's secretary.''

''He's a department head, right?'' Ms. Snippett's gaze darted around the outer office. ''Would my office be as big as this one?''

''More or less.'' Natalie hadn't measured the space, for heaven's sake!

''I won't have to deal with patients, will I?'' the woman continued in a clipped voice.

''Occasionally, although we have a separate office that schedules appointments,'' she said. ''Since you've worked at a hospital, I should think you'd be used to encountering patients.''

''If you'd read my résumé carefully, you'd have noticed that I was in the public-relations department,'' said Ms. Snippett. ''Frankly, the woman I reported to was incompetent. I did such a good job they were about to promote me into her position.''

Instead, they laid you off. Natalie wondered whether the hospital's cutbacks had required Ruth Snippett's dismissal or merely provided an excuse to get rid of an obnoxious employee.

She finished the interview with as much courtesy as she could muster, then made a note to reject the application. There was nothing wrong with ambition, but in this case the doctors would have to hide their scalpels, because otherwise Natalie feared Ms. Snippett might stick one in the back of anyone who got in her way.

She returned to the Barr mansion in a thoughtful mood. Choosing the right person for Dr. Carmichael certainly wasn't easy, although Ms. Liu was looking better and better in retrospect.

On arrival she found Loretta discussing strategy with Patrick, who appeared relaxed and stronger. He'd reserved a massage for lunchtime, as Natalie had suggested, and apparently it had done him good.

It was nearly dinnertime when the public-relations director collected her files and shook hands with Patrick. She and Natalie walked into the foyer together.

"How are you doing?" Natalie asked.

"You mean personally? I'm miserable," Loretta said. "I got my period today. It felt like a slap in the face. Another failure."

Natalie's heart went out to her. "I hate to see this situation tearing you apart."

Loretta hugged her briefcase. "I can't stop thinking how lucky Rita is. I'm delighted for my sister, but it hurts, too. I want a baby so badly, it's affecting every aspect of my life. I've even been snapping at my husband."

She ought to consult with Amy, Natalie thought. But what right did she have to advise the other woman when she couldn't even solve her own problems? "I'm sorry to hear that."

"Oh, never mind me." Loretta produced a tremulous smile. "As my mother keeps saying, it'll happen. I just need to keep my mind on other things in the meantime."

"Good luck." As she watched Loretta depart, Natalie almost wished she'd said something about counseling. If she couldn't figure out a solution to her own situation, she might need some herself. How *was* she going to show up every day for work after the birth and keep pretending to Patrick that it was Ralph's baby she played with, delighted in, worried over and nurtured?

The solution was obvious: She had to tell him the truth. It might not be wise to do so while she was supposed to be taking care of him, since that would make it doubly awkward if he threw her out.

But she should level with him the first chance she got. After all, Patrick moved with greater ease now, and she didn't see why she needed to stick around after tonight.

She said so to Bernie, who brought pizza for dinner. "I suppose you're right." His sister's mouth quirked. "Mrs. Frick will be here tomorrow, so he won't be alone during the day."

Patrick, who was lounging in his seat at the kitchen table, listened to this discussion with amusement. "I'm glad you ladies have worked out the caretaker arrangement. I'd hate to have to muddle through on my own."

"I'll bet you can make it up the stairs already," said Mike, who was pouring a glass of milk for his younger son. "You're probably malingering so people will fuss over you."

"Sure. You wouldn't believe how well I'm eating," Patrick said. "Look at that counter. We've got pies and cakes up to our eyeballs, courtesy of my friends and neighbors."

He wasn't kidding. At his request, Natalie had taken

a couple of desserts to the office earlier, but there was plenty left.

"Can I have more pepperoni?" asked Kent.

"You've had two pieces!" said his older brother.

"Who made you the pizza sheriff?"

"You can both have more," Bernie said, and handed them each a slice.

After dinner, Bernie's family made inroads into a chocolate cake and, at Patrick's insistence, took a pie home when they left at nine o'clock. Patrick and Natalie waved goodbye from the front portico.

"You really are making progress," she said. "When's your next doctor's appointment?"

"Friday. I think he'll pronounce me ready for dancing lessons by then." Still using his crutch, he accompanied her inside. "Has it been uncomfortable staying here?"

"Not at all." Since moving into a bedroom that, judging by the decor, must once have been Bernie's, Natalie had felt at ease. "I miss my collection of rabbits, though."

"I've been toying with an idea." Patrick broke off to stifle a yawn. "Excuse me."

"You've had a busy day." Natalie didn't want to hang around for any lengthy discussions. Being alone with Patrick was becoming increasingly uncomfortable. Even now, she had to fight the urge to touch him. "I'm certainly exhausted. Interviewing secretaries is harder than it sounds."

"Find anyone?" he asked.

"There's one possibility," she said. "I'll tell you about her tomorrow. Right now I'm going to collapse, if you don't mind."

A furrow formed between his eyebrows. "Nat, I've

been selfish this week. It isn't right that you should be working night and day, especially in your condition. If you'd like to take a day or two off after the Oktoberfest, you're entitled to it.''

She didn't want a vacation. Ruth Snippett's casual assumption that she would have to be replaced bothered her more than she'd expected. She could handle her workload just fine.

"I don't need a vacation, because this isn't work," she said. "I love Doctors Circle as much as you do, and I'm glad to help in any way I can. I'll see you in the morning."

"Sleep well."

Half an hour later, Natalie put down her book in disgust and climbed out of bed. She might be tired, but she wasn't sleepy. What she needed was a dip in the whirlpool.

Heather had warned her not to get overheated, but the water temperature wasn't set high, she'd noticed when she'd been in the master bathroom. A brief soak ought to relax her and, since she had the second floor to herself, she doubted Patrick would notice or mind.

Digging in a drawer, she found an old bikini that must have been Bernie's. It fit and, besides, no one was going to see her.

PATRICK WISHED Natalie wasn't so eager to move out, although he hadn't wanted to say so in front of others. Having her here made him realize how big the house was, and how empty, without her.

Their discussion about his parents had been echoing through his brain. As he sat at his desk downstairs reviewing his e-mail, he wondered why he'd never before considered the fact that his father, although absorbed in his work, was sustained by his family's unwavering love.

Also, sharing the house with Natalie these past few days had filled Patrick with a contentment he'd never known before. Perhaps he did have needs he hadn't acknowledged.

There ought to be some way to make them both happy, to provide her with a safe haven for her child and him with companionship. Patrick was sure he could figure out the solution, if only his muscles weren't rebelling from their increased activity.

The effects of the massage were wearing off. What he needed was a trip to the hot tub.

He could climb the stairs if he took his time. In view of Natalie's exhaustion, she'd probably fallen asleep by now, so he didn't want to call for help. Besides, unless he thought of a plan, Patrick was going to be on his own, starting tomorrow. He might as well get used to it.

The first few steps went easily. After that, Patrick had to lean on the railing to avoid putting too much weight on his ankle. He supposed his awkward movements would make his muscles even sorer, but the hot tub should cure that.

On the upper landing, he gazed with satisfaction around the familiar lounge area. Maybe he would resume sleeping up here tomorrow night.

In the master bedroom, he pulled off his shirt and tossed it over a chair. Unzipping his pants, he hobbled into the bathroom and flicked on the light.

A gasp made him snap to attention. Natalie, sitting in the pool spilling out of a very skimpy swimsuit, stared at him with her mouth open.

Chapter Twelve

Natalie's hair was piled atop her head, and a few wisps clung damply to her cheeks. Patrick caught a tantalizing glimpse of her breasts above the bikini before she slid farther into the water.

"I thought you were asleep," he said. "I mean, it was dark in here and you don't have the jets on."

She gestured toward a couple of candles glimmering at the perimeter of the hot tub. "I found these in the vanity and thought I'd enjoy the atmosphere. I'm sorry. It never occurred to me you'd come in."

"Bernie gave me those. I've never used them." Patrick stood there holding up his pants and debating what to do next. He could hardly strip naked, as he'd intended, and slide into the pool. On the other hand, it made no sense for him to flee, either.

"I should go." Natalie didn't move. Apparently she was too embarrassed to step out of the water wearing a bikini, even though Patrick had seen everything there was to see of her on the yacht. That, however, had been nearly two months ago, and things had changed since then.

"There's no reason we can't both enjoy the hot water. Just a minute." With as much dignity as possible,

Patrick retreated into the bedroom and found a pair of swim trunks.

He half expected Natalie to seize the opportunity to scram, but she was still lurking underwater when he returned. "I forgot to bring a towel," she said.

A pile of bath sheets stood on open shelving, but she'd have to cross the bathroom to reach them. Patrick set one near her, but not too close. "Don't leave yet," he said.

On the way upstairs, an idea had formed in his mind. He wanted to broach it tonight, and right now he had a captive audience.

"I guess I'll stay for a while," she agreed. "I don't believe either of us could be any more embarrassed than we are already."

"That's right. Think positive," he joked.

Patrick turned off the lights, leaving only the soft illumination of the candles, before easing gingerly into the hot water. He could see on Natalie's face that she wanted to assist him but was reluctant to touch him.

He was glad she kept her distance, since the mere sight of her velvety, half-naked body was stirring a powerful masculine reaction. Thank goodness for the cloaking power of swim trunks and near-darkness.

Settling in, Patrick found he didn't miss the usual swirl of the jets. He liked the peace of simply resting and letting the heat and candle glow work their spell.

"Congratulations," Natalie said. "You made it all the way up here by yourself. I didn't expect you to do that yet."

"I'm stubborn," Patrick said.

"You're determined," she corrected. "That's one of the qualities I admire about you."

Although other people had mentioned that his secretary spoke highly of him, Patrick wasn't accustomed to receiving direct compliments. He liked it. "Purely out of politeness, I'm willing to let you tell me the other qualities you admire."

"If I did, you'd be insufferable." Her smile appeared as a pearly crescent in the dim light.

"How did I go from having many admirable qualities to being insufferable?" Patrick asked.

"Every good secretary knows how to handle her boss," Natalie said. "In your case, you need an assistant who can stand up to you and tell you when you're veering off course. I can't do that if I'm simpering with adoration."

"Simpering with adoration?" he repeated. "I like the sound of that."

"See what I mean? A few words of praise and your ego inflates like a balloon!"

He ignored the insult. "Tell me more about how you 'handle' me."

"Well, I know you appreciate it when I tune in to the office scuttlebutt, so I try to keep you informed," she said.

"You're my eyes and ears, and I know I can rely on your discretion." Patrick, who didn't want to invade his staff's privacy, trusted Natalie to tell him only about problems or situations that might affect him. "Do you mind?"

"No. I like the fact that you respect my judgment," she went on. "It's a nice change from Dr. Grier. He never valued anyone's opinion except his own."

"He must have been hard to work for." The man had always been polite to Patrick, but then, he'd been a member of the board of directors.

"Very hard," Natalie said. "But not nearly as hard

as Spencer Sorrell would have been. After Dr. Grief retired, I was so glad when you got the job that I was tempted to make a burnt offering on my mother's barbecue.''

''At least my predecessor did one sensible thing,'' Patrick said. ''He hired you.''

''I nearly didn't get the job.'' Natalie's tone changed. ''There's something I've never told you...''

He didn't want discuss Dr. Grier anymore, because this was the perfect chance to bring up his idea. ''There's something I'd like to tell you, too. Please hear me out before you come up with a zillion objections, okay?''

She hesitated, as if considering finishing whatever anecdote she'd started about Dr. Grier, then decided to yield. ''I'm listening.''

''I think you should move in here.''

''You do?'' She leaned forward intently. Candle glow softened her face and played across the cleavage revealed by her bikini.

Patrick nearly forgot what he'd been about to say. It took a moment to dredge up his reasons. ''For one thing, I enjoy having you around.''

''You see me every day in the office. Isn't that enough?''

''No,'' he said. ''You were right about my father. Even though he didn't pay us much attention, he was here for us when it counted. I think that, like him, I might not be cut out to march through life alone.''

Natalie gazed at him with a tenderness he hadn't seen since that afternoon on the boat. It made him feel ten feet tall, and it revved every bit of masculinity in his body.

It also drove all remaining rational thought from his mind.

NATALIE'S CAUTIOUS SIDE warned that she shouldn't give in to the joy welling inside her and that she ought to be on her guard. But Patrick was talking about spending the rest of his life with her. He'd practically asked her to marry him.

She'd been on the verge of confessing everything. When she did, it might drive him away. Right now, she didn't want to think about that possibility.

This was too wonderful. This man, this moment, this admission of caring. Maybe, in spite of everything, they could work things out.

"Hold me," Natalie said.

"We ought to… I mean, we shouldn't…" He broke off in confusion. Oh, how she relished that hopeful, muddled expression on Patrick's face. He was looking to her to make the next move, so she did.

"This is a conversation best conducted while I'm sitting on your lap." She glided across the hot tub and his arms drew her close as if by instinct.

The moment her bottom came into contact with Patrick's lap, she discovered that he was aroused. The hard feel of him against her softness dispelled the last shreds of restraint.

"I've missed you," he murmured in her ear.

"Then let's make up for lost time."

Before, when they'd made love, they'd both been a little shy. This time, Natalie raised her mouth to his without hesitation.

Patrick kissed her thoroughly, demandingly, while his hands removed her top and cradled her breasts. Moments later, the pieces of their swimsuits were floating lazily away.

She traced the length of his body with her own, skin to skin. The effect was almost unbearably sensual. Natalie wanted to go slowly, yet the sensitive points of her body throbbed with yearning as Patrick tasted her throat, the tips of her breasts, then her mouth again.

They flowed together, aided by the water. It kept urging them against each other until he entered her with a smooth upward thrust.

Natalie wrapped her arms around Patrick's broad chest, rested against him and let his forceful rhythm carry her into another dimension. A web of magical sensations spread through her.

She had never opened herself to anyone the way she did to him, never trusted anyone this much. Not even Patrick their first time. In the intervening weeks, it was as if their connection had deepened without either of them realizing it.

He seized her hips and anchored her above him, then drove into her with such fire that she cried out. It was glorious, sheer heaven. Natalie arched her back, and felt him catch her breasts with his lips as his power filled her.

He groaned aloud, and the two of them melted together in a flare of heat so intense Natalie half expected the water to vaporize. When she came to herself, she was snuggled against Patrick amid the quiet rippling of the pool, surrounded by a gentle, candle-softened darkness.

It was the kind of moment, she thought, for saying, ''I love you.'' She waited, hoping to hear the words. When they didn't come, she smiled to herself. For all

Patrick's wonderful qualities, no one had ever accused him of having a glib tongue.

"I didn't expect that," he said a bit breathlessly.

"I'm glad to hear you didn't calculate it," Natalie replied. "Neither did I, in case you were wondering."

He drew her more tightly to him. "I seem to lose control when I'm around you."

"That's a good sign," she murmured against his cheek.

"It is?" He shook his head. "I mean, it isn't. That's not what I had in mind."

"You had something else in mind?" She felt tension creeping through her body.

Patrick lifted her onto the underwater bench beside him. "Remember what I was saying earlier, about you moving in with me?"

"Of course." Natalie could hardly breathe. Had she misunderstood him? But his intentions had seemed so clear.

"Here's the idea I had." He leaned back, putting a little distance between them. "I've got a house full of empty rooms. There's no reason you couldn't move in here with your baby. I'd be like an uncle."

"An uncle?" she repeated, not liking the direction this discussion was taking, even though she'd had much the same thought herself a week or so ago.

"You pointed out how much I enjoy my nephews," Patrick said. "I'm sure I'd feel the same way about your baby. There'd be practical advantages for you in living here, too."

"I always like practical advantages," Natalie said dryly. What she really wanted to do was shake him until he told her that he was crazy in love with her. Instead, she waited uneasily.

"If you're living here, you won't have to worry about finances when you take maternity leave," he went on earnestly. "To minimize gossip, we can convert the downstairs office into a room for you and I'll move my equipment upstairs."

"So we'd be like roommates?" Natalie asked. "People would still gossip, Patrick."

"It's not such a scandalous arrangement," he said. "You know, my mother once talked about having a live-in housekeeper. We could let people assume—"

"A housekeeper?" Fury propelled Natalie to her feet. She scarcely noticed the cool air or the water cascading down her naked body. "That's what you expect from me?"

"No. I said it wrong. Natalie, listen…" Patrick's stricken look told her he was trying to run damage control.

She was in no mood to be patient with the man's verbal fumbling while her dreams shattered around her. She'd been expecting true love, and he wanted a housekeeper!

"It's bad enough that I'm your secretary and I'm sleeping with you without people thinking I'm your servant!" she cried. "Oh, Lord, I can't believe I just said that. I can't believe what we just did."

"Natalie, we can tell people anything you want," Patrick said. "You can say you're renting a room. Or…" He stopped, apparently unable to think of any other explanations than the obvious one—that she was his mistress. Which was all he was offering.

A small voice of reason inside Natalie's head pointed out that Patrick believed she was carrying Ralph's child. Exactly what did she expect from him?

That he would love her so much it didn't matter!

Because she loved him that much, and more. She'd have married him no matter what his circumstances.

It wasn't exactly a revelation that she loved Patrick, but the implications hit Natalie hard. She didn't merely love him, she was on the point of abandoning her pride, of bursting into tears and admitting her lies and begging him to forgive her.

Which he would never do. Because, as he'd once told her, the thing he valued most about a person was integrity. Obviously, if he loved her at all, he certainly didn't love her enough to overlook the fact that integrity wasn't her strong suit.

"I'm going to leave now," she said. "Please close your eyes."

"What?" Despite his evident distress, Patrick started to laugh. "You don't want me to see you naked? After we made love?"

Natalie knew she wasn't the most consistent person in the world. Sometimes her feelings collided with common sense so noisily she wondered that other people couldn't hear the crash. But she felt what she felt. "Just do as I ask, please."

Patrick shaded his eyes with his hands. "Is this good enough?"

"Fine." She snared the floating pieces of bikini and climbed out of the hot tub. When she was safely wrapped in the towel, she said, "I'll leave tonight. First, though, I want to make sure you can get down the stairs safely."

He uncovered his eyes. "Natalie, I must have misstated my case. I never meant to drive you away."

"We'll forget tonight ever happened." Turning away from him, she dried herself. "This discussion and this…you know what…never happened."

"Yes, they did happen." Patrick started out of the water but stopped with a wince as he put weight on his ankle. He braced himself against the lip of the pool and kept talking. "I'm concerned about you having this baby alone. I'm also selfish enough to know how much I'm going to miss you while you're on leave. What I'm suggesting is a solution to both our problems."

"I don't have any problems," Natalie said, "except that I'm an idiot."

She darted out of the bathroom before he could marshal the strength to come after her. She flew across the open landing and into her bedroom, where she pulled on some clothes and threw the rest into a suitcase. In the spare bathroom, she washed out Bernie's swimsuit and hung it to dry.

She didn't want to face Patrick at breakfast tomorrow morning. Bad enough that they had to work together.

When she emerged from the bedroom again, he was waiting, fully dressed and leaning on the banister. "You're really jumping ship?"

"I'll pick you up in the morning, since you can't drive yet," Natalie said. "You're well enough to go into the office."

"I suppose so." A shadow fell across his face. "I wish you'd reconsider."

"I'll collect you at a quarter to eight." She moved past him with her suitcase. "Follow me downstairs. I want to make sure you don't land in a heap."

Patrick limped down. When Natalie turned to check on him, her heart twisted at the sight of his wistful gaze. She almost relented and agreed to stay for the night.

It wouldn't make any difference, though, she reminded herself. She was better off going back where she belonged.

Once he was safely at the bottom, she carted her luggage out the door. And didn't look back.

PATRICK SAT on the veranda trying to figure out how he'd screwed up so royally. He'd made what he believed was a helpful suggestion and it had blown up in his face. He'd only been trying to hold on to Natalie. Why couldn't she see that?

Obviously he'd insulted her, yet he wasn't sure how. In light of her on-again off-again situation with Ralph, he'd believed she would like the idea of keeping her options open while having a secure place to live. Not to mention a live-in doctor for her child.

Making love tonight had been soul-satisfying. He'd never expected to hold her again, and now that he had, the prospect of returning to a hands-off relationship gave him a hollow feeling.

He hoped he wasn't going to lose her completely. It was what he'd feared since they'd first made love, when he'd become aware of how much she meant to him.

Something had changed inside him during these past few days while they'd shared a home. He wasn't clear exactly about what that was, only that it had something to do with Natalie and living together and her baby.

Patrick pushed up from his chair and seized his crutch. He needed to get enough rest to handle a long day tomorrow.

Maybe the problem was that he'd spent too much time away from the office. Once he threw himself back into the whirlwind that was Doctors Circle, surely he'd stop agonizing over matters beyond his control.

Or maybe somehow he'd find a way to bring them under his control, and win Natalie back.

SHE AWOKE at 3:00 a.m. As usual, her subconscious had been putting in overtime while she slept and had come up with an unpleasant but unavoidable truth.

She couldn't go on working with Patrick. The situation was tearing her apart.

Fortunately her churning brain had also arrived at a course of action. Dr. Carmichael needed an experienced, tough-minded secretary, and who was more experienced and tough-minded than she herself?

Coral Liu would do nicely for Patrick. He'd appreciate her quiet manner. True, she wasn't likely to tap into the flow of staff gossip for him and it would take some time for her to catch up on the job's many aspects, but Natalie would be on hand to help.

She hugged herself, wondering how she was going to get through the days without seeing Patrick. But at least she wouldn't have to leave her home at Doctors Circle. And she'd run into him occasionally, which was better than not at all.

Although her mind was made up, Natalie decided to postpone telling Patrick until after the Oktoberfest. That way, he wouldn't think she was merely overreacting to tonight's events.

Next Monday she'd announce that she was hiring herself as secretary to the new infertility chief. Patrick might object, but she knew he wouldn't stand in her way if she insisted.

There was no need to change positions until January. By then, Patrick would have resigned himself to the switch. Natalie only hoped she could do the same.

Chapter Thirteen

Despite the usual last-minute emergencies, including light showers early in the day and a scramble to find a missing group of valets, the Oktoberfest got off to a rousing start. The rain stopped, the droplets evaporated in the dry air, and the valets arrived in a van, ready to park the cars that began streaming in by seven o'clock.

Patrick didn't even know all the important-looking people who swarmed onto his property beneath the glow of mock Chinese lanterns. Loretta Arista, who had a talent for gladhanding, accompanied him on his rounds, introducing him to political and corporate leaders whose names he recognized.

"I don't think Alfred LoBianco has arrived yet." The public-relations director scrutinized the scene when they had a moment alone. She'd been particularly eager to find the computer-game magnate.

"I'm sure he'll be here sooner or later." Patrick took in the crowds at the catering tent, and the people waltzing on an open-air dance floor. Natalie didn't appear to be here either, yet he knew she'd been on hand earlier in the day to aid in the setup.

"How's your ankle, by the way?" Loretta asked.

"You seem to be getting around all right without crutches."

"It's much better." Patrick had swallowed a couple of over-the-counter painkillers as a precaution.

He'd resumed driving the day before, uncomfortable at having Natalie pick him up each morning. At work they'd confined their discussions to business.

Even so, Patrick didn't kid himself. They could never go back to a platonic relationship, and he didn't want to.

His plan, having Natalie move in with him and raise her baby under his protection, was a good one. If she chose not to make love with him again, Patrick would understand. But he wasn't going to leave her to fend for herself now that she and that ex-husband had gone their separate ways.

Finally he spotted her escorting some guests to a place set up on the bluffs for gazing at the view, binoculars provided. A white chiffon dress swirled around her and her blond hair floated in the light breeze.

Before Patrick could head in her direction, however, Loretta grasped his elbow. "There he is!" she said. "Come on. This is the most important person you'll meet tonight."

"You don't have to persuade me." Patrick made a mental shift into director mode.

Alfred LoBianco, head of WiseWorld Global Productions, turned toward them with a smile, and the two men shook hands. The entrepreneur was in his midforties, with thinning hair and a slender build. His owlish glasses gave him a professorial air.

"I like the way you do things," he told Patrick. "This party is a great way for us to meet."

"I'm glad you could make it," Patrick said. "And

let me know whenever you'd like to visit Doctors Circle. I'd be happy to show you around.''

"I've got some free time Monday morning," the man said affably. "How about if I come by around ten and we'll do the tour thing?"

"Sounds like a plan," Patrick said, his hopes rising. Loretta had mentioned the possibility of a large contribution and perhaps an ongoing sponsorship of some special program, as well. "Care to join us in sampling the beer?"

"You bet."

As they strolled toward the bar, he saw Natalie directing a waiter to serve hors d'oeuvres to some new arrivals. She fit in easily as hostess, Patrick thought with a pang. The woman belonged here. Why was it so hard to convince her of that?

Reluctantly he returned his attention to Alfred LoBianco and to his duties as host.

"THERE SURE ARE a lot of rich folks here tonight," Noreen McLanahan told Natalie as the two of them stood drinking ginger ale on the veranda. "Who needs those lanterns? The moonlight bouncing off the diamonds is enough to blind a person."

Considering that Noreen wore a sapphire-and-diamond choker, she meant the joke to be as much on herself as on anyone else. "I just hope they all take Doctors Circle to their hearts and wallets," Natalie said.

"Speaking of hearts, have you noticed the new heartthrob?" The older woman nodded toward a cluster of women. They were gathered around a tall, light-haired man with merry blue eyes. As Natalie watched, the group burst into laughter at something he'd said.

"That's Quentin Ladd, our new neonatologist," she explained. The young doctor had begun work the previous week and was an immediate hit with parents and staff. The exception was Spencer Sorrell, who'd taken a dislike to Quent, perhaps because he'd complained to Patrick about that preposterous list of rules.

"He's a Ladd who's popular with the lasses," Noreen quipped. "I don't blame them. If I were on the right side of sixty, I'd flirt with him myself."

"Who're we talking about?" Amy Ravenna joined them. Tonight she'd twisted her dark hair into a French braid and donned a maroon pantsuit. "Wait, don't tell me. It's Quent, right?"

"He's cute and you're both single," Noreen prompted. "Go for it, girl."

Amy hooted. "Sure enough, I'll seduce him right where he stands. Me and which army of showgirls?"

"I saw you two talking the other day," Natalie couldn't resist adding. "He seemed to be enjoying your company."

"He told me I remind him of his big sister," Amy said. "That's about right, considering I'm four years older than him."

"I'd say you're scared of the competition, but you shouldn't be," Noreen said. "You're gorgeous and sophisticated, too."

"That's me, a woman of the world." Amy seemed to find the idea hilarious. "I'll teach him the ropes, poor naive boy that he is."

The mayor and several council members strolled by and greeted Noreen. She excused herself to join them.

As Natalie gazed over the crowd from the veranda, she tried not to let herself stare at Patrick. Across the lawn, he was quaffing beer with Loretta and a couple of well-dressed people.

There was something commanding about his presence that made him stand out from the people around him. Natalie wondered why anyone would pay attention to Quentin Ladd when Patrick was on hand.

"Your heart's in your eyes, you know," Amy said.

"Oh, dear." Natalie glanced at her friend guiltily. She hadn't confided anything further about her pregnancy and knew Amy must have guessed the truth. "I hope nobody else sees it."

"Noreen probably does, but she knows just how far to push people and when to hold back," the counselor said. "He's the father, isn't he?"

Natalie sighed. "Yes, but he doesn't know."

"You haven't told him?" Amy clucked her tongue in disapproval. "Come on, girl, he's going to find out your condition sooner or later."

"Oh, he knows I'm pregnant," Natalie said. "He thinks it's somebody else's baby."

"What?" Amy appeared torn between mirth and shock. "You have got to be kidding me! How did you possibly arrange for him to think that?"

"Sheer dumb luck."

"Only you, Natalie Winford, could stumble into a situation like this one," her friend said.

"That's not true!"

"It is. You let people take advantage of you, and they weave you right into their messy webs," Amy said. "I'll bet that's what happened, wasn't it? Somebody was speculating about you, and Patrick believed them."

"More or less," Natalie admitted, not caring to bring

Ralph's name into the conversation. "It's for the best, anyway."

Before Amy had a chance to respond, they were joined by Rita Beltran. Wearing a loose silk dress to accommodate her pregnancy, she'd added flowers to her upswept hair.

"You look great," Natalie said, and introduced her to Amy.

"So you're Loretta's sister." Amy glanced at her stomach and added, "Congratulations."

"I'm getting so big, maybe there's more than one baby," Rita said. "I'd be thrilled, but it's hard on Loretta. She doesn't talk about it to me, but she cries on my mother's shoulder all the time. She wants a child so much."

"I think she should talk with Amy," Natalie said. "Infertility is one of the main reasons Patrick started the counseling office."

"It's one of our specialties," Amy agreed. "Maybe you could drop a hint, Rita."

"I couldn't!" The woman shook her head, making the flowers in her hair tremble. "Natalie, she'll listen to you. You talk to her, okay?"

"I'll do my best." From beneath a festive canopy, the band swung into a polka, and Natalie felt her foot start to tap. It was too bad Patrick was in no shape to dance, not that he was likely to ask her to be his partner in front of everyone, anyway.

At the moment he was heading toward the view area with a thin man wearing wire-rimmed spectacles. That must be Alfred LoBianco, Natalie thought. A very important man, except that, right now, she wished he was somewhere else.

She wished all these people would go away. No, she

wished it was Tuesday night again and she was sitting in the hot tub while Patrick wandered in stripping off his clothes.

He'd looked so handsome she'd been overwhelmed, sitting there by candlelight in her borrowed bikini. She'd wanted to hide under the water, or grab him, or do something crazy. Come to think of it, she had.

"Let's go sample the food," Amy said. "I walked by the tent earlier and when I caught that scent, my diet went right into a nosedive. The only reason I didn't stuff myself silly was because I felt duty bound to let other people go first."

Rita smiled. "I'm with you. Frankly, I'm starving."

Natalie went along. The next best thing to true love was chocolate, and she'd seen plenty of that on the dessert table.

THE OKTOBERFEST was described by the local newspaper as a tremendous success. The reporter listed the notables in attendance, described their elegant clothing and quoted from Patrick's short, welcoming speech.

To him the most important part were the pledges of support from a number of participants. The Endowment Fund was edging toward a quarter of the goal.

On Monday morning Alfred LoBianco showed up at ten as promised. He paid close attention while Patrick escorted him around.

"To be honest, I have a personal reason for my interest in Doctors Circle," the computer tycoon said as they drank coffee in the courtyard after visiting the Birthing Center. "My wife and I have an eight-year-old daughter, whom we adore, but we haven't been able to have another child."

"I'm sorry to hear that." Patrick had guessed there

might be some personal reason for the executive's interest. "We're here to help."

"I'm sorry Eva couldn't come Saturday night. Our daughter was running a temperature, but she's fine now." Alfred squinted in the sunlight. "Although I've offered to send Eva to any clinic she wants, she hates to be away from home. We were both ecstatic to hear that Dr. Carmichael will be working so close to us."

"We're all looking forward to his arrival," Patrick said.

"The facilities here are impressive. I want to help." Alfred watched with interest as workmen carried lumber into the wing being remodeled. "I can't promise anything until our new game debuts in November, but let's just say fifteen million isn't out of the question."

Patrick nearly choked on his coffee. Half of the goal! With the publicity that such a huge donation generated, other money would pour in.

"That would be fantastic," he said.

After Alfred departed, Patrick went back to his office to review the center's costs and revenues, as well as to study which areas were generating patient complaints. He liked to keep a close eye on operations.

After five o'clock he became aware of a drop in the level of ambient noise. The construction workers had gone home, as had much of the staff.

To Patrick, this time of day, without ringing phones and drop-in visitors, offered a good chance to play catch-up, and he was glad when Natalie knocked and entered his office. They hadn't found a moment today to speak quietly, which he very much wanted.

"Please sit down," he said.

She edged onto a chair and straightened the hem of

her skirt. Her gaze failed to meet his. "I've decided who to hire as Jason Carmichael's secretary."

Patrick knew he'd done the right thing in turning the task over to her. How typical of Natalie to handle it so efficiently. "I'm glad to hear it. Do you think she's up to dealing with him?"

"Absolutely," Natalie said. "You see, it's me."

He couldn't have heard correctly. "I'm sorry. You said 'me'? As in yourself?"

"That's right." She peered up at him as if expecting a rebuke. "I'm the perfect person for the job. I'm certainly tough enough, don't you think? One of the women I interviewed, Coral Liu, could take over my post here. I'll have several months to train her."

A white-out in Patrick's brain left him speechless. He almost forgot to breathe. After a long moment he said, "You don't want to work for me anymore?"

Moisture glimmered in Natalie's eyes. "I can't. Patrick, this is too hard on both of us. Especially on me. You have to admit, I shouldn't be working for a man I'm having an affair with. Or did have an affair with, even if it was only twice."

"It's not only twice if I can help it." He was making things worse, he saw by the way she drew back. "Forget the past. Let's talk about the future."

Natalie stood up. "This is exactly the kind of discussion I don't want to be having."

"Why not?" Patrick asked.

"Because I can't...we can't..." She threw her hands in the air. "This is why I can't work for you! You keep bringing it up!"

"You mean the obvious?" He leaned across the desk. "Like the fact that—" Patrick stopped cold, shocked by what he'd been about to say.

Like the fact that I love you?

It was so inevitable, he wondered why he hadn't seen it before. He loved Natalie. Yet he'd alienated her so much that she didn't want to work with him.

Patrick couldn't put the pieces together in ten seconds. That, unfortunately, was all the time she gave him.

She backed away. ''I'll provide you with Miss Liu's résumé and my notes about our interview. You might want to talk with other candidates, as well. It's your choice.''

''I prefer the secretary I have,'' Patrick said.

''That's not an option.'' She turned and fled out the door, through her own office and down the stairs. He could hear her footsteps echoing back at him.

Patrick sat there, stunned. When his two previous relationships had crumbled, he'd felt sorrow but also relief at being free to throw himself wholeheartedly into his work.

There was no relief now, only a determination not to give up. Natalie was too much a part of him to lose.

He hadn't realized how much he needed her until they spent time together at his house, away from the office. Until then, she'd been so interwoven with his job that he hadn't seen her clearly.

Maybe she didn't see him clearly, either. What they needed was time together away from work. They needed to date.

That was one social ritual of which Dr. Patrick Barr knew himself to be clueless. However, he wasn't without resources. As a professional man of thirty-eight, he knew when it was time to seek expert advice. Into his mind came an image of the very person to dispense it—his brother-in-law.

Mike had won Bernie, after all. As Patrick recalled, she'd been happily playing the field until then. Mike must have done something right.

It was time for the doctor to arrange a consultation.

NATALIE WAS STILL trembling when she got home. Wrapping her arms around a large, stuffed bunny, she curled up on the sofa.

She'd agonized all day over what she was going to say to Patrick, and even so, it hadn't come out right. She'd stammered like a schoolgirl, unable to give him a clear-cut response that would make him accept her decision.

Of course, how could she? That was the problem. She couldn't come out and say, "I've lied, and I'm still lying, and you're going to hate me when you find out. Can't you see I'm trying not to lose you entirely?"

She reviewed Patrick's responses. Initially they'd been promising. He'd said he wanted to talk about the future, hadn't he? If only he'd dropped to one knee at this point and announced that he loved her, perhaps produced a diamond ring or at least a brochure from which she could make a selection, she'd have been willing to take a chance.

Instead, he'd summarized his feelings by saying, "I prefer the secretary I have."

That was all she meant to him. Well, maybe not quite all, but it was the basis of everything. He didn't want to lose an efficient employee who made his life easier.

From outside she heard the slap-slap of thong sandals climbing the cement stairs. It definitely wasn't Patrick, rushing over to beg her forgiveness. Not that he'd done anything to be forgiven for, except fail to adore her the way she adored him.

"Hey!" called Candy as she thumped the door. Peering through the window, she said, "You're hugging the bunny. This must be serious."

Natalie hadn't realized she made a habit of cradling her stuffed rabbit when she was upset. "I'm okay."

"You're sniffling." Her sister tried the door and, finding it unlocked, stepped inside. "Don't tell me Dr. Perfect died of his injuries."

Guiltily Natalie recalled that she'd never filled Candy in on the rest of the week. "He's fine. How's the tour guide business?"

"I'll tell you in a minute." Candy prowled into the kitchen and Natalie heard the refrigerator door open. Apparently now that she'd given up acting, Candy was indulging her appetite with a vengeance. "Are you saving this cheese for anything?"

"Help yourself."

She emerged with a wedge of brie. "I can't tell you how good this tastes."

A few additional pounds looked good on Candy. She'd struggled for years to keep herself at film weight, which to Natalie, looked anorexic, since the camera added ten pounds. Also, Candy looked healthy and natural in jeans and a T-shirt, instead of her usual trendy clothes, which had been short on fabric and long on baring whatever segment of her anatomy it was popular to flash at the moment.

"I like your new image," Natalie said.

"What new image?" Her sister grinned. "I just can't fit into my wardrobe anymore." She dropped sideways into a chair and draped her legs over one padded arm. "I took out two tours this weekend. The men were utterly charming."

"Did any of them ask you out on a date?" she couldn't resist teasing.

"No, but I flirted a little and they gave me great tips." Candy grinned. "Are you going to tell me why you're hugging the bunny?"

Natalie spilled the whole story. When she finished, her sibling shook her head. "I can't believe my proper sister got into such a mess! This sounds like something I would pull."

It didn't comfort Natalie to think that she was just like the rest of her unconventional family. It only underscored her conviction that she fell short of Patrick's standards.

Maybe if he found out the truth and fired her, she, too, could get a job at the tour company, she mused. Except she doubted it was good for pregnant women to be on their feet all day.

That reminded her of something. "Let's go out for a dinner," she said. "I'm famished."

"Don't die of shock," Candy said, "but I'm paying."

"There's a first time for everything," Natalie said, and put the bunny back in its corner.

MIKE MET PATRICK at the yacht-club bar. The two men chose a table by the wall of windows overlooking the harbor.

Outside in the darkness lights glimmered from moored yachts and sparkled off the water. Opposite them curved the Serene Peninsula, its tightly packed houses brilliant against the night sky. Beyond stretched the vast Pacific Ocean.

"What you need," Mike said after hearing of Patrick's dilemma, "is an ad campaign."

Ask an advertising executive and that was the kind of recommendation you'd get, Patrick thought wryly. "I hope you're not suggesting I rent a billboard to ask Natalie out on a date."

Mike stirred his drink. "I'm thinking more along the lines of winning her through a planned approach. Otherwise, you'll be thrashing around without direction."

Patrick had to concede his brother-in-law's point. "How does a man launch this kind of campaign?"

"When I met Bernie, she was the social belle of the ball and I was a new member of the club. I thought she was dynamite, but so did a lot of guys." Mike's face creased with tenderness at the memory. "I didn't want to just ask her out. That would make me like everyone else."

"I can't ask Natalie out?" How else, Patrick wondered, was he going to get a date with her? They were having enough trouble communicating without him deliberately taking an indirect approach. "What did you do?"

"I softened her up," Mike said. "First I sent a dozen red roses with a note 'From your admirer.' No signature. That piqued her curiosity."

"Natalie might think the flowers were intended for a patient," Patrick said.

"You'll have to adapt the strategy to suit your situation," Mike said. "Next I sent a box of Godiva chocolates. Always choose the best. Again, the note read, 'From your admirer.'"

Patrick nodded. "Then what?"

"I purchased a romantic notecard and wrote inside

it, 'Won't you give me a chance?' When she wasn't looking, I slipped it into her gym bag.''

"Still unsigned?" Patrick asked.

"Absolutely," Mike said. "By the way, if you're considering using e-mail, forget it. There's nothing romantic about e-mail."

"Some people meet that way, I hear."

"Do you want my advice or not?" His brother-in-law checked his watch. "I'll have you know, I'm missing bedtime with the boys for you. We're reading a good book, and I'm dying to know what happens in the next chapter. Never mind. If you two can work this out, it'll make your sister very happy."

"Why?" Patrick frowned. "Bernie hardly knows Natalie."

"Bernie has been predicting the two of you would get married for at least a year," Mike said. "She's already got names picked out for your kids."

Patrick decided not to pursue the subject of children. The fact that Natalie had slept with another man and was carrying his child troubled him, although he tried not to dwell on it. "You haven't finished telling me about asking her out."

"Well, she read the card and checked around the room to see who had left it," Mike said. "There I was, sitting on a lounge chair reading a copy of *Home and Garden* magazine, or maybe that's *House and Garden*. I picked it to make me appear appealingly domestic."

"You wanted to marry her even though you hardly knew her?" Patrick asked.

"Heck no," said his brother-in-law. "I wanted to get her into bed. I had no intention in the world of getting married."

"What changed your mind?" Patrick asked.

"Later, I found out Bernie was waging a little campaign of her own," Mike said. "She completely blindsided me. Before I knew it, I was standing by the altar wearing a tuxedo and watching her float toward me like a vision in white. My head's been spinning ever since."

Patrick's lips quirked at the image of his bedazzled brother-in-law. The odd part was that, instead of sympathy, he felt a burst of envy.

Natalie in a bridal gown. Natalie gliding down the aisle like an angel. Natalie coming home to live with him forever.

Patrick took a gulp of his drink and blocked the tantalizing images. The point was to persuade her to go out on a date.

First things first.

Chapter Fourteen

Patrick didn't want to copy his brother-in-law too closely, but on the other hand, he knew how much Natalie loved chocolate. During his lunch break on Tuesday, he picked up a box of Godivas and wrote a secret admirer note on a Post-it, doing his best to disguise his handwriting.

As he drove back to the office, it occurred to him that Natalie might already have telephoned Ms. Liu. Reluctantly he conceded that he shouldn't interfere.

Much as he hated to lose his secretary, his goal was to put his relationship with Natalie on a new footing, not to manipulate her into working for him again. Exactly what he intended to do once they began dating, Patrick hadn't worked out yet.

This idea of being in love was such a startling discovery, he had to proceed slowly or he'd make a mess. So step one was a date, to be followed by other dates, and then someday, in the distant future—okay, the near future—he might ask her to live with him not as a roommate but as his...as his...

Well, he'd come to terms with that issue later.

At the office Patrick was relieved to see that Natalie hadn't returned yet from her break. The problem was, he couldn't find anywhere on her desk to leave the chocolates.

The Human Resources department, apparently unaware of her decision, had dropped off a stack of new résumés this morning. The mailroom had left assorted envelopes, and packages were piling up. Pharmaceutical companies, makers of baby supplies and manufacturers of hospital goods inundated him, as administrator, with samples in hopes of securing contracts with Doctors Circle, and apparently they'd all decided to send items today.

If he left the box of chocolates amid this clutter, Natalie would never notice it. Baffled, Patrick checked around for a better spot.

Her chair seemed to be the only unoccupied horizontal space. Resigned, he set the gift down there. At least she couldn't miss it.

He went into his office with a sense of nervous anticipation.

PAMPHLETS ON PARENTING and career planning littered the floor of Amy's office, along with little envelopes of heart-shaped candy and coupons for diapers. Natalie downed the last bite of her homemade sandwich and began packing another round of items in a receiving blanket decorated with teddy bears.

"I should make one of these for myself," she muttered as she worked. "I qualify as an unwed mother, too." The two women were spending their lunch hour assembling gift packages for the group of teenaged moms-to-be that Amy counseled one day a week.

"You're not a teenager. You don't need career planning advice, either," Amy said.

"I'm not so sure." Natalie tied another gathered blanket with a yellow bow.

"You figured out that you ought to work for Dr. Carmichael," Amy said. "That was smart. You and Patrick need to put space between you. Like maybe the length of a football field."

"He acted the same as always this morning," Natalie said. "I don't think he cares that I'm leaving."

"At least he didn't sulk," Amy said. "I hate it when men sulk."

"I hate it when I can't figure them out, too," she admitted.

It had been a frustrating morning in many ways. Distracted by thoughts about Patrick, Natalie hadn't been able to concentrate on her work and, against her natural tendencies, had left her desk in disarray at lunchtime.

In addition, she hadn't been able to reach Coral Liu, whose roommate said she was out of town for the week. If the young woman accepted another job, Natalie would be back to square one.

"Oops. I forgot to check my e-mail before lunch." Amy got up and went to her desk. "I try to get back to my patients right away if they have a problem."

"Don't they prefer phone calls?" Natalie asked.

"There are people who think better when they hear the sound of their own voice." Amy clicked on the computer. "There are others who can't communicate until they whip all those chaotic thoughts into some semblance of order on their computer screen. Omigosh! Get over here!"

Natalie went to see. Amy was reading an e-mail from Heather. It was addressed to them both, so Natalie assumed a copy was waiting in her own queue.

"It's a girl!" read the excited message. "My granddaughter, Ginger, was born last night at 10:52 p.m., weighing 7 lbs. 11 ounces, and 19 inches long. And guess what? She has red hair just like mine (see photo)!

"Mother and daughter are doing well, and the father is ecstatic, although unfortunately he's still overseas. I kept updating him during labor.

"Hope everything's going well at Doctors Circle. See you in December!"

Amy clicked the photo. On screen appeared the image of a redheaded newborn with scrunched-up eyes and tiny, perfect hands.

The two friends were so excited they screamed and hugged each other. "I'm only a mother-to-be and she's a grandmother!" Natalie said. "It's hard to imagine."

"I hope we get to see little Ginger in the flesh," Amy said longingly. "I love babies."

"What's all the shouting about?" asked a masculine voice from the doorway. Quentin Ladd stood there, a pirate hat rakishly perched on his head.

"One of our friends had a baby," Amy said, being deliberately vague.

"Right there? Behind the desk?" The young doctor started toward them as if to check.

"Don't step on my stuff!" Amy shooed him back. "And what on earth are you doing in that getup? You look like an extra from a Disney movie."

"I'm trying out costumes for Halloween." Unfazed by her comment, Quent folded himself onto the couch. "I think I should dress up as different people until the big day. It's too dull around here."

"Don't tell me you're going to be trying on costumes for the next three weeks!" Amy said.

"What's wrong with that?"

"Personally I'm waiting to see the thong bikini,"

she said. "Which day are you going to wear it? I want to try out my new digital camera."

"You could send a picture to Heather," Natalie suggested. "So she'll see what she's missing while she's on leave."

Quentin grinned at Amy. "I'll wear one if you will."

"Not to work, thank you," she said.

"I heard you live near the beach," he said. "Maybe we could get together sometime."

The counselor regarded him quizzically. "Are you asking me out?"

"Actually I was looking for someone who likes to ride motorized skateboards, and I know how athletic you are," he said. "There's a rental place on the strand."

"That sounds like a hoot." If there was a trace of disappointment in Amy's voice, Quent didn't appear to notice.

"That's what I like about you." He arose in one fluid motion. "You're a great sport."

After one rap on the open door, Spencer Sorrell's shiny forehead and scowling face appeared. "So this is where you're hiding, Dr. Ladd."

"It's my lunch break." Although Quent spoke calmly, he looked annoyed.

"I wanted to speak to you about this costume nonsense," said the pediatrician. "It's unprofessional and confusing to the patients. Take off that hat."

The young man's eyes narrowed, and Natalie thought he was going to refuse. Then he shrugged and tossed it to Amy, scoring a crooked landing atop her head. "Give your patients a thrill," he said. "It looks cute, by the way. See you later." With a nod to both women, he sauntered out, brushing by the older doctor as if he wasn't there.

Spencer glared at Natalie, although she hadn't said a word. Apparently unable to find a complaint, he stalked away wordlessly.

"He's stored up a lifetime of anger and he's dumping it on Quent," Amy said.

"And me, when he gets the chance," Natalie added.

"I'm really starting to loathe Dr. Sorrell. I wish he *was* moving the Well-Baby Clinic, so it wouldn't be right next door to me anymore." Amy removed the pirate hat and regarded it in amusement. "Then again, if he did, Quent couldn't pop in here so often."

"He likes you," Natalie said.

"As a sister."

"I'm not so sure about that."

"Believe me, that's all it is, and a good thing, too. I couldn't keep up with the office Romeo if I wanted to," Amy said.

It was typical of her to underestimate herself. "I wish you'd believe how attractive you are," Natalie said. "You could drive that man wild."

"I wouldn't know where to start," her friend said. "Nat, I've never had a serious boyfriend."

"Oh, come on! Just because you never got engaged…"

"I never got anything," Amy said. "I'm a thirty-three-year-old virgin. Not entirely by choice, either."

Natalie didn't know what to say. Having married young, she'd never given the subject of virginity much thought. "Are you kidding? I mean, it seems so unlikely."

"It's no joke, believe me." Amy glanced at her

watch. "I'm afraid I've got an appointment in five minutes."

"We'd better clean up. All I can say, Amy, is that the men you've met must have been complete pea brains."

"Don't worry about it," Amy said. "I'm sure someday I'll meet a guy who's gentle and maybe a bit older and willing to be patient with me."

"Not some young hotshot who might be comparing you to his other women, huh?" Now Natalie understood her reluctance to get involved with Quent. "I hope you find this guy soon."

"So do I."

Natalie helped stow everything in a box, then hurried across the plaza to the East Wing. When she came within sight of her desk, her heart sank. More stuff had been loaded on top in her absence, and she hardly knew where to start.

Her mind absorbed in the clutter, she sank into her chair. And leaped up with a squawk.

NATALIE'S SHOUT roused Patrick from his work. He raced around his desk and hurried out, ignoring the residual soreness in his ankle.

She waved a crumpled box of chocolates in the air. "Look at this! Someone booby-trapped my chair!"

"Maybe they couldn't figure out where else to put it," he said, and wondered why Mike hadn't mentioned any snafus in his campaign to win Bernie. Probably because his brother-in-law hadn't made any.

Natalie examined the box. "These are Godivas. They're the best." She frowned. "Is it my imagination or…?" She reached behind her and pulled the Post-it note off the back of her skirt. "Great. I've got a memo stuck to my rear end."

Patrick retreated into his office. Maybe it would be a good thing if Natalie never figured out who her secret admirer was.

No, he wasn't going to give up so easily. As soon as she calmed down, he had no doubt she would enjoy the chocolates. They could both share a good laugh about this.

Patrick was smiling at the memory of Natalie peeling his note off her posterior when Dr. Sorrell stalked through the door. "How can you tolerate it?" he growled. "That woman's desk looks like a junk heap."

"It was clean this morning," Patrick said. "She can't help it if people make deliveries while she's at lunch."

"You have a rather large tolerance for disreputable behavior." The pediatrician glowered. "I suppose you approve of this nonsense of Quentin Ladd's."

"What nonsense would that be?" Patrick instinctively wanted to defend the young neonatologist and had to remind himself that, for all his bluster, Spencer Sorrell was the head of his department.

"He wants to dress up in Halloween costumes all month, and he's encouraging the rest of the staff to do likewise." Spencer frowned at Patrick's framed degrees and certificates on the wall as if he considered them bogus. "It's undignified. He had no business showing up in a pirate hat without my permission."

"I agree with you," Patrick said. "Costumes may be acceptable on Halloween itself, but parents with sick children won't be reassured to see the staff parading around in them all month."

Spencer's jaw worked, giving the impression he was

almost disappointed not to receive an argument. It soon became apparent, however, that the pediatrician had simply been working up to making another demand.

"He's still on probation," Spencer said. "I want him fired before things get out of hand."

"Is there a problem with his work?" Patrick asked. "Have clients complained?"

"It's our job to prevent trouble." The pediatrician took a defiant stance, feet apart, arms folded and jaw thrust forward. "He's a loose cannon with a disrespectful attitude."

"He's a doctor and, judging by his references, a good one," Patrick said. "I'm sure he expects a certain amount of leeway in his personal conduct. Granted, he's got an excess of youthful exuberance, but—"

"An excess of youthful exuberance? You're good at making excuses for employees, aren't you, Doctor. Like your secretary, who 'can't help it' that her desk is piled sky-high. Or is your personal relationship interfering with your willingness to discipline her?"

Patrick didn't know whether the pediatrician had guessed about the relationship or listened to gossip, but it was inappropriate to throw it in his face during a professional discussion. He felt steam forming beneath his collar. "Natalie has never been less than outstanding in her work. The fact that she was willing to work from my home last week is an example of that."

The pediatrician sniffed as if at a bad odor. "She comes from a white-trash family and she has an insolent attitude," he said. "Her kind doesn't belong at Doctors Circle. If you were a real administrator, instead of a rich boy who got his job because of his connections—"

This attack went completely over the edge. Patrick

smashed his fist on his desk, startling the man into silence. "I want you to get a thorough medical checkup, Dr. Sorrell. I'm hoping there's some medical explanation for your offensive and unacceptable remarks. And let me tell you, if I had to choose between Natalie Winford and you to be on my staff, I would unquestionably choose her."

For a moment he thought the older doctor was going to throw a punch. Patrick was so furious he would almost have welcomed the chance to resolve the dispute physically.

"You haven't heard the last of this," the pediatrician growled, and marched out of the office.

Patrick released a long breath. He was glad now that neither of them had stooped to fighting. And he truly hoped Dr. Sorrell would get help, because either he was undergoing some kind of breakdown or he'd allowed years of petty resentment and frustrated self-importance to turn him into a hopelessly bitter man.

Doctors Circle didn't need an intramural feud. If it came to public attention, it could hurt the Endowment Fund campaign. Even if not, it was bad for staff morale.

How ironic that Spencer believed Patrick had used connections to get the administrative job! In reality he'd only sought it from a sense of duty and accepted it after the search committee presented him to the board as its first and only choice.

Putting the unpleasant incident out of his mind, he returned to work. It was after six when he emerged and saw Natalie clearing the last pieces of mail from her desk.

"I'm sorry about the mess," she said.

"It wasn't your fault." He saw that the open box of

chocolates, which sat on the outer corner of her desk, was half-empty. She'd evidently been sharing it with visitors.

"A lot of that stuff was toys and other items for the Christmas season. I took them over to Miriam so she can see if she wants to carry any of them in the gift shop," Natalie said. "They should have been sent to her directly." The center's policy was to donate items not used in the gift shop to needy children.

"Companies think it's more effective to target the administrator." Patrick didn't want to talk about business. He didn't want them to be leaving separately, either. "Why don't we pick up some dinner?" It wasn't a formal invitation, but it might qualify as a date.

Natalie gripped the edge of her desk. "It would add fuel to the fire if we're seen in public. I heard what Dr. Sorrell said."

"I'm sorry about that. He can be a real jerk."

"Everybody knows I was staying at your house. Most people think it's no big deal, but the less we're seen together, the better," she said. "It's hard, trying to convince people there's nothing between us when…" She stopped.

"When the truth is that we have a relationship," Patrick finished. It had struck him as she spoke that while Mike's approach might have worked for his situation, it was misguided here. What he and Natalie needed was frankness, not games. "We care about each other and we need to acknowledge it."

A look akin to panic crossed her face. "Sleeping together again was a mistake."

"No, it wasn't," Patrick said. "Getting involved

with your ex-husband again, that was a mistake. Please tell me it's completely over.''

''As far as I'm concerned, yes,'' Natalie said. ''But as for Ralph, I can't figure out who else would have pulled a stunt like leaving chocolates on my chair.''

''I did.'' Patrick hoped he wasn't turning red.

''You?'' Her eyebrow quirked.

''It was a dumb idea,'' he said. ''I was trying to be romantic. I guess it isn't my style.''

''It was sweet. No pun intended,'' Natalie said. ''But, Patrick, this isn't going to work. We're better off...I mean, the two of us can't...''

''Maybe we can,'' he said. ''It's complicated, with the baby coming, but not impossible.'' Then he said the most difficult words he'd ever uttered in his life. And the most wonderful. ''I love you.''

She gazed at him as if she didn't dare believe what she'd heard. ''You do?''

''I only feel fully alive when I'm with you.'' Now that Patrick had declared his feelings, he didn't want to stop. ''You're the most honest, caring woman I've ever met. I'd trust you with my life.''

Tears glittered on Natalie's lashes. ''What if I told you that...'' She swallowed. ''Patrick, I need to think. Can we talk about this tomorrow?''

''Of course.'' She looked so vulnerable that he wanted to scoop her into his arms right then and there and take her home. But she'd asked for time, and rushing her was unfair.

It was only after she left that Patrick realized why she must be hesitating. She was afraid he couldn't accept her child because it wasn't his.

He'd walked to work today, instead of driving, and he let the matter play through his mind as he ambled through the Birthing Center building and out the back. At the rear driveway, a woman and newborn baby were waiting with one of the Circle Guild volunteers. Patrick paused to watch as a car stopped and a man hurried out.

Beaming, he took the baby in his arms. The pink-wrapped little girl yawned and nestled against him. Tenderly the man lifted her into the rear of the car and leaned down to strap her into an infant seat.

A yearning burned inside Patrick. If only Natalie's baby was his, instead of Ralph's. Why had she wasted her time with that man? Yet, if she hadn't, there wouldn't be a baby at all.

With a jolt he faced a truth he'd hidden from himself. He wanted to be the man taking his wife and baby home. He had enough room in his heart for both of them.

Loving Natalie meant loving her child, despite the fact that it wasn't his. Patrick had grown up with a Norman Rockwell image of what a family was supposed to be, a mom and dad and two or three kids who resembled them. But it didn't have to be that way.

He could love kids who came from a different background or ethnic group or race. He could even love a child who looked somewhat like Ralph.

Tomorrow he'd explain that to Natalie. Then there'd be no more reason for her to push him away.

Patrick continued walking, and whistled all the way home.

Chapter Fifteen

Natalie was unlocking her car in the parking garage when she saw Loretta wave vigorously from her reserved spot nearby. She waited while the woman strode over.

Natalie could see she'd been crying. "Is something the matter, Loretta?"

"No, not at all. In fact, the opposite. It's good news." Despite her denial, Loretta sounded tense. "My sister had an ultrasound today. You're not going to believe this—it's triplets!"

"I'm thrilled for her." Three cute little babies! A multiple pregnancy could be tricky, however. "It's too bad Heather's not here."

"Oh, Rita loves Dr. Sentinel. He's a bit reserved for my taste, but she says he provides excellent care." Loretta fiddled with her purse. "It's wonderful, after she's waited so long." Apropos of nothing, a tear ran down her cheek.

Natalie remembered her promise to Rita. "You need to get help. This situation is making you miserable."

"I can't do anything until Dr. Rourke gets back," Loretta said. "Or maybe I should wait until February when Dr. Carmichael arrives. I think what I need is a new approach. We've been trying for seven years, and sometimes I don't think I'll ever have a baby.'' She grabbed a tissue from her purse to stem the tears.

''I didn't mean you need medical help, I meant you should consult Amy,'' Natalie said. ''Infertility is really hard on a person. That's one of the reasons we have counselors, as you know.''

''I don't need a shrink, I need a child!'' Loretta wailed. ''Oh, listen to me! I sound like a complete numbskull.''

''No, you don't,'' Natalie said.

''I can handle this.'' Loretta turned away to hide her tear-streaked face as a car passed by. ''I don't know what got into me today.''

Natalie decided to try a different tack. ''Has it occurred to you that stressing yourself out might be making your problem worse?''

''You think so?'' Loretta blew her nose.

''Anxiety can become a secondary cause of infertility.'' She'd heard Heather say so once. ''Even after the original condition clears up, tension can interfere with, you know, the whole process.''

''I suppose that's true.'' The tears stopped. ''At least it would give me something to do for the next few months. I'm going to go crazy if I have to sit around and wait.''

''Call Amy tomorrow,'' Natalie said. ''That is if you want to.''

''Sure, I like her,'' Loretta said. ''She's such a down-to-earth person. Thanks, Natalie.''

''Good luck.''

Natalie mulled over the conversation on the way home and hoped her advice would take effect. Not until she got to her apartment and closed the door did she let her mind drift back to what Patrick had said.

He'd told her that he loved her. It was impossible. It was also thrilling.

Natalie had the feeling that if she gave him any encouragement, he'd ask her to marry him. Marry Patrick! The idea sent a quiver all the way down to her ankles. A second later it reached her toes.

There was nothing she wanted more in the world, but she'd been lying for too long. She couldn't take the next step until she cleared the slate.

Torn between fear and longing, Natalie plopped onto the sofa and hugged her big stuffed rabbit. She'd never been a coward. When it came time to break up with Ralph, she'd faced him down even when he shouted and threatened her. She'd never let the temperamental Dr. Grier intimidate her, either.

Today Patrick had surrendered to emotions he must have been fighting for some time. He'd gone to the trouble of buying chocolates and writing a secret-admirer note. Then he'd made a passionate declaration of love.

Natalie wasn't going to let him down. She had to prove herself worthy by telling the truth. All of it.

She squeezed the bunny tight.

PATRICK COULD HARDLY WAIT to get to work the next day. All night he'd been reexamining his discovery about wanting a child, and he was eager to share his thoughts.

However, he should have known better than to think he and Natalie could have a leisurely talk first thing in the morning. She was tied up on the phone when he arrived and held out a package to him.

Patrick took it with scarcely a glance. He was more interested in checking out his secretary's new style, with her hair pulled back on one side and secured by an enameled comb. The sophisticated look suited her, he decided.

She hung up and, before he could compliment her, said, ''I got overzealous about clearing off my desk yesterday. Miriam sent that one back from the gift shop. It's for you.''

Puzzled, Patrick reached inside the padded envelope and lifted out a videogame. ''Global Oofstinker'' was printed on the cover in bright-red letters over the image of a large-footed cartoon skunk kicking a globe into orbit. ''I'm afraid to ask who this is from,'' he said.

''Read the fine print,'' Natalie advised.

The manufacturer was WiseWorld Global Productions. ''Alfred LoBianco's company,'' Patrick said. ''It's strange to think that the financial security of Doctors Circle may rest on how well a game called Global Oofstinker fares in the market.''

''That was Loretta on the phone. WiseWorld's publicity director wants to drop by this morning to discuss a tie-in,'' Natalie said. ''Apparently these computer types like to work on the spur of the moment.''

''A tie-in?'' Patrick repeated.

''They want to publicize the fact that proceeds will benefit Doctors Circle,'' she said. ''I'll let Loretta explain it. She'll be here in a few minutes.''

The morning flew by. LoBianco's publicity director was a hip but rather goofy young fellow. Patrick and Loretta politely discouraged the man's wilder ideas and agreed on a short, dignified reference to Doctors Circle in press releases and ads.

Not until lunchtime did he come up for air. He was

about to go ask Natalie to eat with him when Spencer marched into his office with a file folder clamped under one arm and a smirk on his face.

The man's innate unpleasantness struck Patrick afresh. "Can I help you?" he asked.

"I have something you need to see." Spencer dropped the file onto Patrick's desk. "Right now."

He picked it up. "Personnel—Confidential" was stamped on the front. When he read the tab, he was surprised to see the name Winford, Natalie. "This is privileged information."

"Open it to her job application," the doctor said. "It's very interesting. Especially the part where she says she was never arrested."

Despite his disgust at Spencer's prying, Patrick couldn't ignore the potential for a serious problem. He opened the file and read Natalie's neat, familiar handwriting.

"Yes, I see where she's answered 'no' to the question about arrests," he said. "We no longer ask that question, by the way. The only thing that concerns us is convictions."

"A lie is a lie, and who knows what else she concealed?" Spencer said. "I took the liberty of running this by my brother. It turns out Ms. Winford was arrested for stealing a car. Finn also recalls that she was picked up as a juvenile, although he doesn't have access to the details."

"Juvenile records are sealed for good reason—to give kids a fresh start," Patrick said. "As for the car business, just a minute." He went to the door. "Natalie, would you come in here, please?"

She entered the room, regarding Spencer warily. One glance at the application and her face paled.

Patrick wished he could reassure her. However, under the circumstances, he had to act as the administrator, not as her friend and lover.

"Dr. Sorrell claims you were arrested for stealing a car," he said.

"Ralph and I were in the middle of a divorce and he got mad because I canceled our joint credit cards," Natalie said. "Although his name was on the registration papers for our car, I'd always had the right to drive it. He withdrew the claim after I spent a few hours in jail."

"Nevertheless, you lied about being arrested," Spencer said.

"Yes, because I hadn't done anything wrong," she said.

Spencer refused to be put off. "We have a policy at this center of firing employees who lie on their applications. Besides, I'm sure if we check further, we'll find something else you've falsified." He scanned the document. "What about this secretarial certificate? Can you produce it?"

She didn't answer, and Patrick's spirits plummeted. He didn't care whether Natalie had gone to secretarial school, but he knew Spencer would make a federal case out of the matter.

Besides, it was distressing to discover that Natalie, whom he'd trusted completely, hadn't been honest on her application. Much as he hated to give any credence to Spencer's accusations, the falsehoods did raise questions about her character.

"I completed most of the courses, but I was short one. It was about correct office behavior and grooming," Natalie said. "I didn't see why it mattered when I had all the necessary skills and I needed a job. I know

I shouldn't have lied, but I was young and the question took me by surprise.''

Although her lips trembled, her chin came up. Patrick admired her spirit.

Spencer gave a snort of triumph. "I insist you get rid of her at once, Dr. Barr. From now on, I expect you to listen to me. In fact, I don't see why I shouldn't go to the board with what I've learned, to show your poor judgment. If you're smart, you'll follow my lead from now on, starting with firing Dr. Ladd."

Patrick didn't miss the implication that he was being blackmailed into giving Dr. Sorrell carte blanche. That was not going to happen.

"You haven't explained how you got your hands on a confidential file," he said. "Did someone in HR give it to you?"

The man harrumphed. "That's immaterial."

"As you've just pointed out, it's my job to identify improper conduct by the center's employees," Patrick said. "It appears that you've gone snooping for dirt on someone you don't like. You should have come to me if you had reasonable grounds for suspicion. Who else's papers have you poked through? Quentin Ladd's? Mine?"

"If I'd found anything wrong, I'd have brought it in," Spencer said.

"So you admit you looked." It amazed Patrick that the man couldn't see how serious his transgression was. "I need the name of whoever gave you access to those records."

"No one," the man said. "I have a passkey."

"You have a passkey to the entire complex?" No one but the director and the head of security were entitled to those keys.

"Dr. Grier was grooming me to be his successor. He had a copy made so I could familiarize myself with the operations," Spencer said.

This was even worse than conning or bribing an employee. "For five years you've had a passkey to which you aren't entitled, and it never occurred to you to give it back?" Patrick closed his eyes briefly. "You realize we're going to have to perform a complete audit."

"Don't be ridiculous," the man said. He sounded less confident than before, though.

"You know as well as I do that a medical center is responsible for every controlled substance and every record about those substances that passes through our facility," Patrick said. "We thought we knew who had access to what. This is going to cost a lot of money and I'm going to have to bring it before the board."

He was exaggerating for effect. Doctors Circle performed regular audits already, but still, had there been any real suspicion of theft or tampering, a large-scale assessment would certainly be warranted.

Stunned, Spencer blinked several times. From his expression, Patrick could see that he was searching in vain for excuses or counteraccusations.

"Here." The older man fished in his pocket and handed over the key. "I give you my word that this is the first and only time I've used it. You know that nothing irregular has turned up in any of our departments, and it won't, either."

"At the very least, we'll have to change all the locks." That should have been done long ago, Patrick acknowledged silently, but he'd never imagined that Dr. Grier would be so irresponsible.

"I couldn't lose my medical license over this, could I?" Spencer asked tensely.

"That would depend on what we find. If there are any discrepancies, you'll be an automatic suspect even if they're not your fault, because of that passkey," Patrick said.

"I never considered...surely you wouldn't..." His mouth worked like a fish gasping for air. Despite the trouble Spencer had created, Patrick felt a stirring of sympathy. The man was in his sixties and had devoted decades to his work. Now he stood to lose everything.

That didn't change the fact that he'd tried to blackmail Patrick and deprive two people of their jobs. Also, his penchant for troublemaking made him a threat to the center's reputation. Allowing him to remain was unthinkable.

"Let me make a suggestion," Patrick said. "Doctors Circle doesn't need a scandal. I'm willing to keep the matter quiet if you'll submit your resignation. Of course, should it turn out you *have* used this key improperly, I'd have to go to the authorities."

"His brother is chief of police," Natalie put in. "You can't expect him to take action."

"Finn would pillory me if I broke the law." Sweat beaded Spencer's forehead. "He'd take it as a reflection on him."

"I'll expect your resignation before the end of the day," Patrick said.

The older doctor's face was a study in conflicting emotions. At last he said, "I've been telling my family for years that I want to retire and play golf all day. I guess this is as good a time as any." His eyes narrowed and he jerked his head toward Natalie. "What about her?"

"I'll deal with my secretary as seems appropriate to me," Patrick said. "She isn't your concern."

Spencer released a breath. "You'll have my resignation right after lunch." Leaving the file behind, he slunk out of the room.

"I'm sorry," Natalie said when they were alone. "Believe it or not, I was going to tell you that stuff today. It's why I kept putting you off. We couldn't have a relationship until I came clean, and I was afraid to."

"You were afraid of me?" Patrick didn't know what to make of this revelation.

"Yes, in a lot of ways." She looked thoroughly contrite. "Afraid I'd lose my job, but even more afraid I'd lose your respect. I should never have let things get so out of hand. It's my own fault."

Much as he wanted to forgive and forget, Patrick felt shaken. He'd made his policy about honesty well-known and had fired another employee for lying. More than that, he was no longer sure he knew Natalie very well.

He'd never suspected the real reason she was keeping him at a distance. Even now, he only had her word for the claim that she'd planned to make a confession.

"Is there anything else you haven't told me?" he asked. "I don't want more surprises later."

From the way she averted her gaze, he realized she was still holding something back. What now?

"You'd better sit down for this one," Natalie said.

"I'm fine right here." He braced himself against the edge of his desk.

Her clear blue eyes regarded him wistfully. "It's about the baby."

"Is something wrong?" His heart thudded.

"No, it's…well, Ralph isn't the father," she said. "You are."

Her words rattled through Patrick's skull. From downstairs, he heard the thwack of hammers and the buzz of saws. From outside, he noted that the choir was practicing at the Serenity Fellowship Church. The song was ''Sometimes I Feel Like a Motherless Child.''

This child not only had a mother, but two fathers. Or rather, a very astonished single one.

''Please explain to me why it seemed like a good idea to lie about that,'' Patrick said.

Natalie hugged herself. ''I wish I had my bunny here.''

''Excuse me?''

''Never mind,'' she said. ''Ralph gave you the impression that he was the father—inadvertently, I guess. When I found out you believed that, it kind of let me off the hook, or so I figured in my own confused way.''

''Which hook would that be?'' Patrick asked, still too numb to sort out how he felt.

''It meant I didn't have to come clean and risk losing you forever,'' she said. ''I figured it was better to keep working together and see you in a limited way than to admit what an idiot I'd been and antagonize you permanently.''

''You certainly had a lot of faith in me,'' Patrick said dryly. ''I wouldn't have turned you out in the street like some waif in a nineteenth-century novel. Natalie, what kind of jerk do you think I am?''

''I don't think you're a jerk. I didn't want you to feel obligated to marry me, either.'' She squared her shoulders, gathering courage. ''But I know you walk the straight and narrow, and if life is a balance beam, I've fallen off too many times to count. You have a policy of firing employees who lie, and that policy applies to me, as well as to anyone else. Right?''

"I suppose so," Patrick conceded.

"No matter how much you try, you'll never understand how badly I needed this job six years ago," Natalie said. "I've been a good secretary and you know it. If I'd told the truth, Dr. Grier would never have given me a chance."

She had a point. But if every employee invented his or her own rules, if integrity meant nothing as long as a person had a good enough excuse, where did it stop?

"I have an obligation as director to put aside my own feelings," Patrick said reluctantly.

"You're going to fire me?" Her voice quavered.

With his mind in such turmoil, he didn't know how to proceed. "I have to give this some thought," Patrick said. "There's a lot at stake, especially with a child on the way. You know I'll support you both."

"You'll do the honorable thing." Natalie's mouth twisted. "I respect that about you, Patrick. I just wish…" She hesitated.

"What?"

"That we'd met under other circumstances. But then, if we hadn't been working together, I doubt we'd ever have met at all. So I guess the lies were worth it." With an apologetic shrug, she slipped out the door.

Looking around his office, Patrick reflected that nothing about it had changed in the past hour. Yet inside him, everything was disarranged, smashed, wrecked.

And yet, he was going to be a father. It was the greatest gift he'd ever received, and he knew already that he would love his child with every breath he took.

The only problem was that, depending on what

course he took, he wasn't sure the mother would ever speak to him again.

NATALIE WAS SO DISTRAUGHT that she went to her mother's trailer for dinner. When she discovered that the menu consisted of frozen pizza and lima beans, she nearly changed her mind, but tonight she needed to talk to someone who was neither a straight arrow nor judgmental.

"So I told Patrick he's the father, but I think he's going to give me the sack," she finished her story.

"I knew you wouldn't sleep with Ralph." Angie hiked up her apron, which had one strap hanging by a thread, and shook her bushy hair. She'd dyed it purple this week. "I hope this doesn't mean the gift shop is going to stop carrying my dolls."

"Patrick wouldn't be so petty," Natalie said.

Clovis set jelly-jar glasses of water on the table. "You could help your mother make dolls. The business is really growing."

"I might have to," Natalie said. "If they let me go without a reference, I don't know how I'll get another job."

"Not to mention that you're pregnant," her mother pointed out. "By the way, I heard from your brother Bill." He was the one who'd lost touch since joining the navy.

"How's he doing?"

"He got married," Angie said. "To an Italian girl. He says she's an architect. They're coming to visit next spring, when he finishes his tour of duty. Then he says they might go live near her family. I don't know what he'll do in Italy, but he's learning the language."

"Ciao," said Clovis. "Andrea Bocelli. That's all the Italian I know."

"Maybe I'll go live there, too," Natalie said. "It can't be any harder to find a job there than here."

She didn't mean it, of course. She wanted Patrick to know his child. She wanted him to forgive her, and maybe someday, long after he fired her, she'd be able to forgive him, too.

She just wished tomorrow would come and go quickly.

Chapter Sixteen

In contrast to the cool October air, the pool felt warm when Patrick sliced into it. He'd been venting his tumultuous emotions by exercising for the past half hour, and his muscles hummed pleasantly.

He climbed out, water dripping around him, and remounted the board. A half twist in a piked position had been one of his favorite dives when he was young. As he went through the motions now, Patrick remembered the day he'd first mastered it and how excited he'd been to show his father.

"Dad! Come see my new dive!"

"Sure thing. Go ahead. I'll be watching."

He'd hurried onto the board at the swim-team's pool, determined to perform perfectly. And he'd dived cleanly and sharply, to the applause of his teammates. Coming up, pumped with enthusiasm, Patrick had looked for his father's reaction.

Joe hadn't seen him. He'd been too busy scribbling in his notebook, absorbed in a new idea.

The old disappointment darkened Patrick's mood as he surfaced. Surely by now he should have forgotten that incident, or at least stopped experiencing the same letdown whenever he remembered it.

With his own child, Patrick vowed silently, he wouldn't make the same mistake. Of course, he had to spend long hours at work, but there was nothing he'd enjoy more on the weekends than paying attention to his kids, whether they were executing difficult dives or simply sailing a toy boat around the pool.

What made him different from his father wasn't just his attitude, Patrick conceded with a rush of contrition. Unlike Joe, he didn't have to work his way up from poverty. The older man's sacrifices had paid for the education that freed Patrick from the crushing need to work constantly.

As he climbed out and slung an oversize towel around his shoulders, a rush of love for his father swept over him. Until now Patrick had never considered his childhood from an adult perspective. Faced with becoming a father himself, however, he could see that Joe had behaved as he did from noble motives.

Patrick had been apprehensive about parenthood because he'd believed his obsession with work would make him repeat Joe's negligence. But it wouldn't. He was a different person with different goals and opportunities, thanks to his father.

In fact, once the Endowment Fund drive ended and he'd done his best to sustain his parents' dream, he was going to return to pediatrics. There would still be pressures and hard work, but he'd love what he was doing.

A weight lifted from Patrick's soul. He strode toward the house, filled with excitement about the unexpected vistas opening before him. A return to the career he loved. The impending birth of a child who was already becoming central to his hopes and dreams.

What about Natalie?

Upstairs in his room, while changing clothes, Patrick replayed images from their times together. Natalie soaking wet, her hair clinging to her cheeks, her lips full and eager. Natalie pulling him down atop her, her skin sliding against his, her movements enticing.

He hadn't even tried to resist, either on the yacht or last week. He'd landed himself in this tangle by ignoring his responsibility as her employer. Patrick was equally, perhaps even more, at fault than she for putting them in this awkward situation.

Yet that didn't excuse Natalie for lying to him about the baby. Worse, she'd done it to cover up her initial lies, piling deception atop dishonesty. Patrick didn't see how he had any choice but to abide by hospital policy.

It was going to break his heart. Maybe even more than it would break hers.

In the stillness of the room, the ring of the phone startled him. Patrick picked it up. "Hello?"

"Mike told me about your campaign." It was Bernie. "How'd it go? Did you win the fair lady?"

"I'm afraid not." If he had to confide in someone, it might as well be his sister. "It turns out she'd lied on her job application. I'm going to have to let her go."

"You're going to fire Natalie?" Bernie squawked. "I can't believe she'd do anything seriously wrong."

"She didn't, frankly," Patrick said. "But we have rules."

"Oh, for Pete's sake!" wailed his sister. "I was hoping you'd grown up, but you're as rigid as ever."

"Rigid?" The word choice puzzled him. "I never knew you thought of me that way."

"Stiff-necked, uptight and a real pain the whole time we were growing up," Bernie said. "I admit, sometimes I admired those qualities, especially when other people were going along with the crowd and acting stupid. But you never knew where to draw the line.''

"I always knew exactly where to draw the line," Patrick insisted.

"Remember your friend Alan?" Bernie said. "After he cheated off your test paper, you refused to speak to him again."

"What he did was wrong. He got me in trouble, too." The principal had grilled Patrick for an hour before accepting his word that he'd known nothing about the cheating.

"I know, but then it turned out his parents were having a nasty divorce and he was going through meltdown," Bernie said. "It was cruel the way you wouldn't forgive him."

"I couldn't bring myself to, not at first." Patrick had to admit, though, that he'd come to regret his harshness. "I did try to make up with him later."

"By then he'd switched schools and started running with a bad crowd," Bernie reminded him. "It was too late."

"I didn't cause his problems," Patrick said.

"You could have helped him."

"I wish I had," he admitted. "We were both inexperienced kids. This is different. I'm the head of a medical center, and Natalie's an adult. I can't think of my personal feelings."

Bernie gave an audible sigh. "There's no point in arguing. I'm right, but you won't figure it out until too late."

"Since you've believed you were right in every argument we ever had, I won't take that prediction too seriously," Patrick said. "Please give my thanks to

Mike for trying to help. It was interesting to find out how he maneuvered you into dating him.''

"He didn't maneuver me," his sister said. "I knew he was the secret admirer all along."

"Why didn't you say anything?"

"What, and cut off the flow of candy and flowers?" she said. "Besides, I was impressed. Being organized and paying attention to detail made him good husband material, and the fact that he went to so much trouble meant he really cared about me. Maybe more than he knew."

"That's an interesting observation," Patrick said.

"I hope you and Natalie get back together." Bernie clicked her tongue. "If you blow this one, bro, don't come crying to me. Wait—I just remembered that you saved my life recently. Okay, you can cry on my shoulder if you want to."

"I'll keep that in mind," he said.

Only after they'd hung up did it strike Patrick that he'd forgotten to mention the baby. Well, he would save that important topic for another time.

Patrick wished he wasn't the administrator and that disciplining Natalie was someone else's problem. But he'd never shirked his duty before, and he wasn't going to do so now.

Still, his discussion with Bernie played through his mind as he got ready for bed. How rotten he'd felt when he realized he and Alan could never be friends again...the fact that Mike's attention to detail showed how much he cared, even if he didn't know it...a romantic campaign...

It was almost enough to keep a weary man awake. But not quite.

THE NEXT MORNING nostalgia gripped Natalie as she walked from the parking garage between the Birthing

Center and the West Wing. It was hard to imagine that this chapter in her life was coming to a close, after all the challenges and changes she'd weathered.

Natalie felt so much a part of Doctors Circle she couldn't imagine not coming here every day. To her, establishing the Endowment Fund was more important than her own precarious financial future.

She wanted to watch Jason Carmichael join the staff and see how he got along with Heather. She wanted to find out what happened to Cynthia and her twins, and whether Loretta ever got pregnant, and how Rita fared with her triplets. Hearing about them at a distance wouldn't be the same as seeing everything firsthand.

As she entered the courtyard, a couple of staff members waved and a volunteer called a cheery hello. Putting on a pleasant face, Natalie greeted everyone as if she hadn't a care in the world.

No matter what happened, she didn't intend to skulk around like a criminal. She wasn't going to give up her friendships with Amy and Heather, whom she knew would be loyal. Also, she expected to have her baby here, since it was the best facility in Serene Beach.

As for Patrick, Natalie supposed he'd be too uncomfortable to want to remain friends, although of course he'd visit the baby from time to time. The ironic part was that she admired his uprightness. The fact that he himself would never have kept a key to which he wasn't entitled had given him moral weight in his confrontation with Spencer.

Yes, she respected him. She also wanted to give him a swift kick for throwing away the most precious relationship in both their lives.

Until Patrick came along, Natalie had never dreamed she could enjoy simply being near a man. And that afternoon on the yacht, she'd discovered her own sensuality for the first time.

There would never be another man like him. She didn't want there to be. Every time she looked into her child's face, she would see Patrick and love him all over again.

When she reached her desk, the phone was ringing and interoffice mail spilled from her in-basket. No matter how early Natalie came in, other people always seemed to be on the job, too.

Patrick arrived a short time later, talking intently with one of the senior pediatricians. From the snatches of dialogue Natalie overheard, they were discussing how to redistribute Spencer's patient load until a replacement could be hired.

The news of Dr. Sorrell's resignation spread like wildfire. Staffers began dropping by Natalie's desk, asking if it was true and probing for details. She pretended to have no idea why he'd departed so abruptly to spend time on the golf course.

By tomorrow, after she got fired, they'd all have a fresh subject for gossip, she reflected unhappily. Eventually, when word got out that Patrick was the father of her baby, the grapevine might overload altogether.

It was midmorning when Patrick buzzed and asked her to come into his office. Natalie's throat constricted. Childishly, she felt like running away. Instead, she picked up her steno pad as always and went in.

Her mind insisted on clinging to hope. Maybe, after a night's sleep, Patrick had changed his mind about firing her. Perhaps he was only going to reprimand her or discuss another matter entirely.

One glance at his tense expression and Natalie stopped dreaming. He didn't look angry, but he didn't smile, either. He came around his desk and waited while she closed the door behind her.

"Did you reach Ms. Liu about the secretarial job?" he asked when she turned to face him.

At the reminder of her replacement, Natalie struggled to hold back a defiant tear. She didn't want to embarrass herself in front of Patrick. She'd done enough of that yesterday.

"Her roommate says she's gone until the weekend," she said huskily.

"I see." Patrick frowned as someone tapped on the door. "Yes?"

Miriam James peeked in. "Sorry to disturb you. Where should I put these?" She was carrying a vase of red roses and baby's breath, one of the most expensive arrangements carried by her gift shop.

"Set them on the table there, please," Patrick said. Shyly the shop manager obeyed and slipped out, closing the door behind her. "Sorry about the interruption. Where was I?"

"We were talking about Ms. Liu." Natalie's throat was so dry she could hardly get the words out.

"Oh, yes. Well, that'll have to wait until Monday, then. Now, I've been going over the hospital's personnel policy." He stared past Natalie at the wall. He hadn't even asked her to sit down, she thought unhappily. "I presume you've read it?"

"I helped revise it a few years ago," she said.

He ducked his head in acknowledgment. "Sorry. I'd forgotten." He'd asked for her input and given her the rough draft to edit four years ago, when he and the personnel director updated them. "The appropriate section doesn't say that lying on an application is automatic grounds for dismissal, but—"

Someone else knocked. His forehead creasing in annoyance, Patrick called out, "Enter!"

A young deliveryman hauled a large box into the office. It bore cartoon images of babies, a trademark of a nearby children's shop called Yes! Kidding. "I was told to bring this in here," he said.

Natalie started to tell him to leave the box outside in her office. Her throat clogged.

"Leave it by the door," Patrick said, and gave the man a tip. "Where were we?" he asked when they were alone.

You were about to fire me. She wasn't going to help with her own demise, however. "Personnel policy," Natalie said.

"That's right." Patrick reached onto his desk and picked up a sheaf of papers as if to refresh his memory. For heaven's sake, why was he wasting so much time going over the details when they both knew the outcome? "It talks about dishonesty or deception in matters of substance."

"I know," she said.

"In my opinion, your arrest record doesn't qualify as a matter of substance." Patrick leafed through the policy. "The secretarial certificate I'm not so sure about."

"The only thing I lacked was a frou-frou course in office conduct," Natalie said, then wondered why she was bothering to defend herself in the face of a foregone conclusion.

The door opened without preamble. A college-age girl poked her head inside. Balloons printed with the word "Congratulations!" floated around her. "Like, I guess these go in here, right?"

Natalie bit back the urge to scold her for intruding.

It wasn't her job to protect Patrick from these people any more, or it soon wouldn't be.

"I'll be needing those later." Handing her a tip, he secured the balloons to the back of a chair.

"See ya around." The girl ambled out.

Patrick returned his attention to Natalie. "Back to matters of substance. I've come to the conclusion that you're right. Since we no longer require a secretarial certificate for a candidate with the right skills, I don't see this as a matter of substance, either."

"But you fired a lab technician for lying about his qualifications," she blurted, then wished she'd left well enough alone.

"He lied about having been fired from his last job," Patrick said. "The reason he was fired was because he stole drugs. One of the pharmacists spotted him lingering in an area where he wasn't authorized, and that's what made us check him out. If he hadn't been caught, he'd probably have stolen drugs from us, too."

"I see." Natalie supposed she should be relieved, but Patrick didn't look as if he'd finished, so she waited uneasily.

"That leaves the issue of your lying to me about Ralph," he said.

That, Natalie conceded silently, was indeed a matter of substance. How ironic that, if only she hadn't tried to conceal her other mistakes, she'd be safe now. "It was wrong. I shouldn't have taken the easy way out."

"That's right, you shouldn't have." Patrick glanced up as the door, which the balloon girl had left ajar, opened farther.

"Are you Patrick Barr?" asked a uniformed man carrying a small package. Receiving a nod, he said, "Sign here, please."

Patrick scribbled on the man's clipboard and accepted the packet. Another tip changed hands and the fellow departed.

Natalie blinked, but she hadn't been mistaken. The package bore the logo of the town's best jewelry store. Flowers, toys and balloons poured onto the premises daily, but she couldn't recall the last time Serene Gems had made a delivery.

"Who's that for?" she asked after the messenger left. "Oh, I remember. It's Bernie's birthday next week." She kept track of Patrick's important dates and had reminded him of this one a few days earlier.

"Oh, that's right." He jotted a note on a pad. "It slipped my mind."

"I thought—"

"Let's get back to Ralph." At the mention of her ex-husband, Natalie forgot what her question had been. "Maybe I shouldn't have been so quick to believe he was the father just because he talked about how much you wanted a baby, but I can't believe you kept the truth from me. Were you really planning to raise my child without ever telling me?"

Natalie decided that, perhaps belatedly, she ought to be honest. "Yes." His flinch filled her with shame. Well, she ought to be ashamed, shouldn't she? "At least, I might have. I don't know if I'd have gone through with it."

"I always pictured you as stable, forthright and dependable." Patrick drummed his fingers on the edge of the desk behind him. "Maybe that's why it took me so long to see past the surface."

Natalie couldn't stand here any longer. She knew how much she'd disappointed Patrick. He could never forgive her, he didn't want to work with her anymore, and even if there hadn't been a hospital personnel policy, she'd proved herself unworthy of his trust.

"You don't have to say it." She squeezed her spiral pad so tightly the metal coils dug into her skin. "I know what I did was unforgivable."

"Actually…"

She couldn't stop or she'd burst into tears. "I'll type up my resignation right now. I'm sure you don't want me sticking around when this is all so embarrassing."

Patrick tried again to interrupt, but Natalie was drowning in a flood of words. "You don't have to fire me. I know that's awkward for you, and that's why I'm resigning, not because I don't want to have to put on my next résumé that I was fired. I'm not that calculating, even if I am a liar. I just kind of seize on opportunities, or I let them seize me, and look what a mess I've made. I wish I could promise that I've learned my lesson, but sometimes telling the truth isn't as simple as it sounds. Oh, what on earth am I talking about?"

When she stopped speaking, Patrick remained frozen, staring at her as if struggling to unravel the twisted course of her announcement. Great, now she'd made an even bigger fool of herself.

"I'm going home," Natalie said. "I'll type up my resignation and leave it in your desk." She half ran from the room.

Her vision was too blurry with tears for her to clean out her desk, and besides, she didn't care what happened to all those old breath mints and packets of tissue. She grabbed her purse and sprinted for the elevator.

PATRICK REMAINED standing in front of his desk, trying to puzzle out what had made Natalie react so severely. In matters of business or medicine, his mind worked rapidly. When it came to sorting out emotions, however, it took a while, and today Natalie's emotional state seemed to him unusually complex. Just like his own.

Minutes ticked by. Before he could reach any conclusions, shouts issued from downstairs. Patrick's heart leaped into his throat at the fear that something had happened to Natalie.

He dashed out of his office, nearly colliding with the director of nursing and the chief financial officer, who'd come from their offices to see what the noise was about. From below wafted the acrid scent of smoke.

Personal matters vanished from Patrick's mind. He took the steps at top speed, sore ankle or no sore ankle.

The construction foreman met him at the bottom. "Nobody's hurt. One of the welders started a small fire," he said. "It's under control, but we've called the fire department as a precaution."

Patrick registered the approach of sirens. He hadn't paid any attention to the sound before because it was common to hear ambulances bringing women in labor.

"How bad is the damage?" he asked.

"It's mostly smoke," the man said. "I've given the men the day off. We need to let this air out."

"I'll get our insurance agent out here right away." Patrick stopped to greet the fire battalion chief heading through the door. "Apparently the fire is out."

"We'll take a look for ourselves," the man said. "Is anyone injured?"

Patrick and the foreman answered questions and led the firemen to the site of the mishap. There was no more time to worry about Natalie, not for hours.

Chapter Seventeen

Dear Dr. Barr,
Due to the circumstances we discussed this morning, I am resigning my position as your secretary.
By the way, what do you want to do about the
baby?

Natalie erased the last sentence from her computer
screen. She couldn't mention her pregnancy in the letter, which would be placed in her employment file. On
the other hand, how could she leave Patrick with a
cold, impersonal note, as if they meant nothing to each
other?

He'd certainly behaved decently this morning. Now
that she had the leisure to review what he'd said, Natalie decided he'd been more than generous.

He'd forgiven her for lying on her résumé. He'd also
been polite about that Ralph business, when he had
good reason to be angry. What an awkward position
she'd put him in!

Remembering the scene in front of the Barr mansion,
when Patrick had withdrawn to give her privacy with
Ralph, Natalie felt the blood rush to her cheeks. The

only reason he hadn't thrown the oaf off his property was that he'd believed the man had fathered her baby.

But in the end it all came down to the same thing. He'd been on the verge of firing her when she lost her nerve and ran.

Outside, she heard light footfalls on the stairs. She closed the computer file so no one would accidentally read her letter.

"It's me!" Amy called through the screened window.

Natalie let her in. "Word sure gets around fast."

"What word?" said her friend. "I saw you hotfooting it across the courtyard and figured you and the boss must have had a blowup. I'd have been here sooner, but it took a while getting through all those fire engines."

"What fire engines?"

"From what I heard, one of the welders started a small fire right about the time you left. Don't worry, it was out almost as fast as it started." Amy prowled into the kitchen and opened her sack lunch on the table. "Mind if I eat? It's my lunch break."

"Go ahead. I'll join you." Natalie wasn't hungry, but Heather had advised her to eat regular meals. She slapped together a sandwich and sat across from her friend.

"So what happened with Patrick?" Amy asked.

Natalie filled her in. "He was preparing to can me, so I quit."

"You can't quit!" the counselor said. "You run that place. We all depend on you."

"Not anymore," Natalie said sadly. "Oh, Amy, I should have known it would end this way. It just kills me to admit Chief Sorrell was right. I don't belong in that job and I certainly don't belong with an important man like Patrick Barr.''

"What is this—self-pity? That's not like you," Amy said. "You're just being insecure, you foolish girl."

"No, I'm not." Natalie had trouble swallowing a lumpish bite of her sandwich. Maybe peanut butter hadn't been the best choice in her present state of mind. She gulped some milk before continuing. "It was hopeless from the start. Patrick would never have looked at me twice if we hadn't worked together, and now I've violated every rule he holds sacred."

"I can't believe he's going to let you go," Amy said. "The man's desperately in love with you."

"Really?" Natalie's spirits rose. "If anyone should know, it's you."

"Why do you say that?"

"You're a psychologist. You have all this insight into the human heart. It must be wonderful. You can practically look at somebody and read his mind."

A piece of Amy's corned beef must have gone down wrong. She sputtered and coughed, and couldn't speak for several minutes. When she could, she said, "I am so clueless. You have no idea."

"About Patrick?" Natalie asked.

"About men," Amy said. "I can help a patient sort out his or her emotions, but in daily life, I'm worse than hopeless. I have so little experience with men there are thirteen-year-olds who could give me lessons."

Natalie forgot her own predicament in the face of this confession. "I know you're a virgin, but that doesn't make you ignorant about men."

"From a romantic perspective, it does. All my life,

I've been every guy's kid sister. Now I'm Quent's *big* sister, and that's no better.''

"He likes you," Natalie said.

"Not the way you think. We went roller-skating on the boardwalk yesterday after work. Lots of women flirted with him and he flirted right back. Afterward he asked me how I liked this one and that one, like I was his best buddy.''

"There are worse things than being a guy's best buddy," Natalie said. "Like being his ex-secretary.''

"At least Patrick's attracted to you!''

"If Quent isn't attracted to you, he must be blind.''

"It isn't a person's looks that count, it's what she does with them." Amy crumpled her sandwich wrappings and stuffed them in the empty bag. "I move like a boy. You know that swishy-swaying thing women do with their hips?''

"No," Natalie replied.

"That's because you do it instinctively, which I never could," her friend said. "You should see yourself from behind—on second thought, forget I said that. Anyway, there were all these babes trying to pick up Quent, and I felt like his maiden aunt.''

"You're the one he asked to go skating," Natalie said.

"That's because he hasn't made any guy friends on the staff yet." Amy rested her chin in her palm. "I'm sorry, I didn't come here to talk about myself. You're the one with the major problem.''

"Thanks for reminding me." Natalie's troubles crowded back into her thoughts. "Maybe I should leave town entirely. I'll bet my brother Max would put me up in Las Vegas while I look for work.''

"You can't run away! It's cowardly.''

"You don't have to put up with sneers from the chief of police and a lot of other people," she said.

"Chief Sorrell wouldn't dare sneer at you," Amy said. "Everybody figures there's a story behind Spencer's sudden departure. You couldn't have pried him out of that job with a crowbar if he hadn't done something wrong."

"That's what they'll say about me, too," Natalie said. "And don't forget the baby. My situation is going to be real obvious in another month."

Amy sighed. "I'd like to continue this discussion, but I've got to see a patient in fifteen minutes. Natalie, don't give up. I'm counting on you to be brave and on Patrick to uphold my faith in men."

"I'm not going to kid myself," Natalie said. "However, in deference to you and the fact that I can't figure out what to write in my letter of resignation, I'll postpone turning it in until first thing tomorrow."

"That should give him enough time to come to his senses," Amy said.

"Dreamer," said Natalie.

BY QUARTER TO SEVEN that evening, following a nap and a lot of procrastination, she printed out her brief letter of resignation. Despite what she'd said to Amy, Natalie decided that, if she waited until morning and delivered it to Patrick in person, she might humiliate them both by bursting into tears.

Better to put the letter on his desk tonight, along with her office key. He'd find them first thing tomorrow morning.

Her decision made, Natalie felt anxious to get it over with. Patrick usually left by six-thirty, so she figured it was safe to go now. Okay, she admitted silently, she was cutting it close, but in her present, reckless mood, taking risks felt right on target.

She hurried downstairs, past the first-floor apartment where the new residents played their stereo too loud, and climbed into her green hatchback, then shot away from the curb. En route to Doctors Circle, Natalie had to force herself not to weave in and out of the poky traffic moving south along Serene Boulevard.

At least there weren't many cars entering the parking garage. Natalie rounded a pillar and headed for her reserved spot, right next to...

...the space where Patrick was loading the baby-decorated box into his trunk. Balloons surged around him, defying his efforts to tamp them into place, while the bouquet of roses sat on the concrete by his feet, in peril of being knocked over.

"For heaven's sake, you're going to pulverize those flowers!" As soon as she parked, Natalie hopped out. "You should put them in the front seat and secure them with the belt." They must be for Noreen McLanahan, she mused, remembering that Patrick had taken the elderly lady a bouquet once before.

At the sight of her, his dark eyes brightened and he flashed a grin. What was he so happy about? she wondered.

"I don't dare let go of the balloons," he said. "I think they're trying to escape."

Natalie marched to his side. "I'll hold them down while you wedge in the package, okay?"

He made no move to obey. "You came back." In the quiet garage, she became aware of his shallow breathing and the way his body angled toward hers.

She dug in her purse and thrust an envelope, slightly

the worse for wear, into his free hand. "I promised to put my resignation on your desk, remember?"

Patrick's eyebrows knitted. "That's what this is?"

"Correct."

He released the balloons, allowing them to float free, and tore the envelope in two. Instinctively Natalie grabbed the knotted strings and stopped the ascent. "What did you do that for?"

"You have no reason to quit." For want of a trash basket, he stuffed the remnants of her resignation into his trunk. "I wasn't going to fire you."

"But I lied on my application!" She heard her voice echo through the garage. "And about Ralph!"

"The latter was a personal matter," Patrick said, "nothing to do with your job. The former, as I said before, is not a matter of any substance. So..."

Natalie got a funny sensation, standing there anchoring a bunch of balloons imprinted with the word *Congratulations!* "You mean I still work for you?"

"Darn right you do," he said.

"Are you mad because I took the afternoon off?" She'd never done anything like that before.

"I just wish I could have come by your place sooner," Patrick said.

"What do you mean, sooner?"

"That's where I was going now." He scooped up the vase of roses. "These are for you."

"Really?" Natalie clasped the vase, savoring the lovely fragrance.

"So is the stuff from Yes! Kidding." Patrick indicated the paper-covered package. "The saleslady helped me pick out a layette set, a diaper stacker and a whole assortment of items you'll need. Consider it a baby shower in a box."

"Wow." Natalie wasn't sure what to make of all this largesse. "What about the balloons? What are you congratulating me for?"

"Those got delivered a bit early," he said. "Wait a minute." He patted his pants pockets. "Where did I put it?"

Natalie knew Patrick well enough to figure that, whatever he'd misplaced, it was in his jacket. "Try a little higher."

"Right." From his inner coat pocket, he drew out a velvet jeweler's box.

The delivery from Serene Gems had been for her? This had to be a dream, which meant Natalie was still taking her nap.

"This seems so real," she said.

"Excuse me?"

"I can smell the flowers," she said. "The balloons kind of squeak when they rub together, did you notice? I don't usually have dreams this intense."

"You're wide awake. By the way, is there motor oil on the floor?" He peered downward. "I can't tell with this poor lighting. You're always so observant."

His question about oil made perfect sense if Natalie was dreaming. Otherwise, it came completely out of the blue. Nevertheless, she looked down. "I don't see any."

"Good." Patrick dropped to one knee. Even for a dream, this was odd behavior.

"You'd better get up before anyone sees you," she said. "What would they say?"

"They'd think I was proposing to the woman I love, and they'd be right." He opened the jewelry box to reveal a ring that, despite the dimness, sparkled with diamonds. "Natalie, I'm sorry I made such a botch of things earlier. I was trying to pave the way logically, which was a really illogical idea, because love has nothing to do with common sense.''

''You're proposing?'' she said in astonishment. ''That's what you were leading up to?''

''At the risk of repeating myself, I love you.'' Patrick smiled. ''I guess I took you for granted, or I took my feelings for granted, until I nearly lost you. Will you please, please marry me?''

''Pinch me,'' Natalie said.

''That's probably the strangest answer a man ever received to a proposal.'' Patrick arose and, as usual, towered over her. ''How about if I kiss you, instead?''

''That would be nice.'' As one arm encircled her waist and his mouth came down on hers, Natalie barely hung on to the balloons and the flowers.

The kiss deepened slowly and sweetly. Patrick's strength soothed the last of her fears. He held her against him for a long moment as their hearts beat rapidly.

He drew back a few inches. ''I'm waiting for my answer.''

Natalie took a deep breath. ''Yes,'' she said. ''I would marry you on any planet in the universe, in any state of mind, waking or sleeping.''

She wasn't certain, even now, that this was happening, until she heard Noreen McLanahan say, ''Let me be the first to congratulate you.''

Natalie and Patrick turned, caught off guard by the older woman's approach on rubber-soled shoes. ''Thank you,'' he said.

''I was sitting in my car listening to a CD.'' Noreen indicated her Cadillac, lodged a few dozen feet away in a slot reserved for the board of directors. ''When I saw you two talking, I decided to lie low rather than interrupt. But I'm going to be late for my stint in the gift shop, so forgive me for barging in.''

"There's nobody we'd rather tell first than you," Natalie said.

The gray-haired woman beamed at them. "I promise not to blab to anyone until you make a formal announcement. You two young lovers have made my day. And my evening. When are you getting married? I've got to buy a new dress."

"We haven't—" Natalie began.

"December," Patrick said. "I'd like for us to be married before Christmas. Is that okay with you, Nat?"

"Sure," she said. "As long as we can have the ceremony at the Serenity Fellowship Church. I'd love it if the choir sang for us."

"I'll arrange it right away," he said.

"Let me know if there's anything I can do to help." Grinning ear to ear, Noreen bustled off. There were going to be lots of cheerful faces when the news got out, Natalie thought. She was glad Spencer wouldn't be around to spoil the mood.

"There is one more thing I need to tell you," Patrick said.

"Could we do this over dinner?" Natalie said. "I'm starving."

"Absolutely," he said.

Although neither of them was dressed up, he drove her to the finest French restaurant in town. This being Southern California, the maître d' didn't bat an eye at her rumpled shirtwaist dress or at Patrick's knees, which unfortunately had picked up a little oil, after all.

Over fillet of sole (his) and shrimp scampi (hers), Patrick said, "Once the fund-raising campaign is over,

I intend to go back to pediatrics. That might mean leaving Doctors Circle.''

''You'd be perfect for Spencer's job,'' Natalie said.

''It might make things awkward for the new administrator, whenever we hire him or her,'' Patrick replied. ''But I'll think about it. Would you mind the change?''

''Not as long as I can be your secretary,'' she said.

''You won't have to work.'' The candlelight brought out golden glints in his eyes.

''I'll have to help out at least part-time,'' Natalie said. ''You'd be lost without me.''

Patrick reached for her hand under the table. ''You got that right.''

''THAT'S THE CUTEST baby I've ever seen!'' Amy sat cross-legged on the carpet, cradling the red-haired newborn. The infant examined the counselor's finger in fascination.

''She puts all other babies past and present to shame,'' Heather said proudly.

Although her leave didn't end for another month, the obstetrician had brought her family back to her town house. The new mother and daughter would stay with her until February or March, when Olive's fiancé was expected to return from overseas.

''Thanks for the compliments.'' Olive reclined on the couch, her freckled face glowing with happiness. ''Ginger's a sweetie, aren't you, little girl?''

The baby glanced toward her mother's voice and cooed. Natalie's heart turned over. She could hardly wait until she held her own child in her arms.

That was a few months off, however. In the meantime, she had a wedding to put together. Only six weeks away. Her engagement was exactly one week old and, with all the fuss after they'd announced it at work, this Thursday evening had been the first chance for the women to get together.

"I hate to mention it, but we've got to make some decisions," Natalie said.

Her sister Candy set down a plate of cream-cheese-filled celery sticks from which she'd been munching. "I am not buying one of those ugly bridesmaid gowns that you never wear again."

"You're the maid of honor," Amy said. "You can pick something different from Heather and me. Personally I like those weird dresses. It's an American tradition."

"The only thing that concerns me is the color." Heather shuddered. "Some shades look hideous with red hair. Are you doing the big, white dress thing, Natalie?"

"My sister Alana's sending her gown from Oregon," Natalie said. "We're the same size and it's gorgeous." At Alana's wedding, it had looked straight out of a storybook.

"It really is fantastic," Candy agreed.

"Let's all go dress-shopping together this weekend," Natalie suggested. "The next question is, what about the reception?"

"I vote for the Birthing Center cafeteria," Amy teased. "What could be more romantic?"

"Patrick could book a banquet room at the yacht club," Heather said.

"Too elitist," Candy retorted as she nibbled on a cheese cracker.

"Actually, I have an idea, but I wanted to run it by you guys before I laid it on Patrick," Natalie said.

"You know that huge holiday reception he hosts every December?"

Staff and patrons from Doctors Circle streamed through the mansion over the course of an afternoon and evening, consuming gallons of eggnog and helpings of food from a lavish buffet. The house was professionally decorated with an enormous Christmas tree, holly, mistletoe and a profusion of lights. An orchestra played holiday tunes and, at the conclusion, Santa Claus distributed gifts to the children.

"That's the highlight of the season as far as I'm concerned," Amy said.

"It's magnificent," Heather agreed.

"Here's my idea," Natalie said. "Why not make that our reception? We'd only have to add a few people to the guest list, and Patrick has a standing arrangement with the caterer, decorator and musicians, so I wouldn't have to try to find people in a hurry."

"You're brilliant," Candy said. "Besides, I've heard so much about that party I was ready to get a job changing bedpans just so I could attend."

"Sure you were." Natalie laughed at the idea of her giddy sister taking on such a down-to-earth job.

It was too bad, she thought, that Coral Liu wouldn't be joining the staff until January, which meant she'd miss the party. The young woman, who'd seemed so reserved during her interview, had let out a whoop when Natalie informed her she was being hired as Jason Carmichael's secretary. Well, with luck she'd still be around for the party next year.

"I wholeheartedly support combining your wedding reception and the holiday party," Amy said. "If we're voting, I vote yes."

Natalie hoped Patrick would see things the same

way. Since they'd agreed not to discuss their personal planning at work, she'd have to wait until tomorrow night, when they'd be handing out candy for Halloween.

The notion of taking over the annual party did seem a bit presumptuous. Since her teen years, the Barr mansion had been a landmark in Serene Beach, a kind of fantasyland to a kid from the trailer park. Simply being invited to the party her first year on the job, when the event was hosted by Patrick's parents, had been an awesome experience.

Society people might consider doubling up her reception with a staff party a bit tacky. Natalie sighed. She'd just have to make the suggestion and see how Patrick reacted.

Combining their lives wasn't going to be easy. She hoped that someday she'd truly be able to feel at home in the Barr mansion, but that day seemed a long way off.

Chapter Eighteen

Every Halloween, following a tradition started by his parents when he and Bernie were young, Patrick chose a theme for the front of his house. This year, it was Cats, Cats Everywhere.

Silhouettes of cats prowled along the top of the portico, backlit by spotlights. Images of Garfield peered from the windows, while on the front porch sat a large pumpkin carved with a cat face.

Patrick, having decided it would be undignified to wear a cat suit, had settled for a half-mask plus pointy ears. He'd left work promptly at five today to get ready. The Barr mansion might require a long trudge up the driveway, but it drew large numbers of kids, because Patrick handed out full-size candy bars.

Natalie had promised to change clothes and arrive by five-thirty. It was quarter to six now and she still wasn't there.

As he emptied a giant bag of chocolate bars into a cut-glass bowl on a table near the door, Patrick wished they were already married. This week, as congratulations flooded in, he'd felt Natalie withdrawing slightly. The attention seemed to make her uncomfortable. The sooner they got past this stage, the better.

He smiled as, through the etched glass of the front doors, he spotted a green blur pulling into the parking bay. A moment later, a large, gray rabbit bounced up the front steps.

Patrick swung open the portal. "Hi, Bugs."

"I know the theme is cats, but I'm always a bunny on Halloween." Natalie looked adorable, her cheeks painted with whiskers and her hair tucked beneath a furry hood. "It's my trademark."

"No problem," Patrick said, and after removing his mask, pulled her into his arms. "As long as this rabbit doesn't mind being affectionate with a feline."

"Don't smudge the makeup," she warned.

He decided to save his welcome kiss for later. "Okay. Well, brace yourself for the onslaught. The kids should start arriving any minute."

Natalie padded inside and stood with head tilted, regarding the two-story height of the entrance foyer. "It's so…imposing."

"This weekend, why don't we start fixing up one of the bedrooms as a nursery?" Patrick asked. "That's the first order of transformation."

"You're planning a transformation?" Natalie frowned, or at least, he thought she did. With all that makeup, it was hard to tell.

"I'm going to have the pool covered and fenced." Its openness was visually appealing but had always struck Patrick as hazardous. He wasn't going to put his child at risk of drowning. "As soon as the baby's born, I'll drain the whirlpool, too."

"That's wise. Still, it has such fond memories for me," Natalie said.

"For me, too." Patrick patted her furry shoulder. "I

promise not to make any changes without consulting you. It's your home now, too.''

''Not really,'' Natalie said.

''I know you don't want to move in until after the wedding.'' They'd both agreed to be discreet, even though her pregnancy was the worst-kept secret in Doctors Circle history. ''But you're going to be the lady of the house.''

She hugged herself protectively. ''I've always been in awe of this place.''

''You'll get over that,'' Patrick said.

''I'm not so sure.'' She took a deep breath. ''Tell me what you think of this idea—I'd like to combine our reception with the holiday party. Is that unreasonable? I mean, it's the Barr family's event.''

''You're part of the Barr family now.''

Her eyes widened. ''Me?''

''We're going to be married.''

''I know, but I'm not the same as you and Bernie,'' she said.

''Why?'' he demanded. ''Because your parents didn't have money?''

''Well, partly,'' she admitted.

''Neither did mine,'' he said. ''Not when I was little.''

''But your father earned a fortune. He built all this, and Doctors Circle, too. My family...well, society people in Serene Beach look down on them.''

Now he understood why she'd been pulling back. Deep inside, Natalie hadn't yet absorbed the fact that they were going to be equal partners in this marriage. She felt intimidated by her new position.

''Natalie, the money and the house don't mean anything to me unless you share them,'' Patrick said. ''You belong here as much as I do.''

''I'm not so sure about that,'' she said.

''I am. As for the reception, if you don't mind Santa going ho-ho-ho on your wedding day, it's fine with me.'' Before Patrick could reassure her further, he had a disquieting thought. ''Of course, you realize there's one guest you might not want—''

Outside, high-pitched voices chorused, ''Trick or treat!'' The bell rang three or four times in rapid succession.

He admitted a bevy of costumed cuties. His favorite was a little girl in a ballerina dress, but a tiny boy in a cowboy hat came in a close second.

Natalie distributed bars into assorted bags and plastic pumpkins. ''Happy Halloween!'' After the visitors left, she said, ''What guest?''

''I always host the top city officials and their spouses,'' Patrick explained. ''I know you're not fond of Chief Sorrell, but it would be hard to exclude him.''

Her nose wrinkled. ''I'm not sure how Angie will react.''

''Your mother has a right to feel comfortable on her daughter's wedding day,'' Patrick said. Angie had not only welcomed him as a prospective son-in-law, she'd asked him for dinner on Sunday. He was looking forward to the oddball menu choices he'd been warned about.

''The chief goes out of his way to be rude to her and Clovis,'' Natalie said.

''We won't invite him unless you want him there.'' If the chief was displeased, he had only himself to blame.

The bell sounded. ''Trick or treat!''

A group of school-age youngsters thrust out their

bags. Superheroes predominated among the boys, with tiaras and princess gowns popular among the girls.

Patrick distributed the candy. By the time he finished, another group was approaching, and this time Natalie did the honors.

When they were alone, she said, "You'd really risk offending Chief Sorrell?"

"If he treats your family rudely, he can't expect to attend your reception," Patrick said.

Her rabbit ears wiggled, and he realized she was chuckling. "Can't you picture it? Chief Sorrell and his wife deferring to my mother in the receiving line? Having to thank me for inviting them? I wouldn't miss it for the world!"

"Then we'll invite him?" Patrick tried not to show his relief.

"You bet!"

A stream of children cut off further attempts at conversation. Half-a-dozen bags of candy later, the rush slowed to a trickle. By seven o'clock, there were no more children in sight.

"That was fun," Patrick said as he switched off the porch light. He'd never enjoyed handing out candy at Halloween this much before, not even when he let his nephews help.

"All those kids!" Natalie sagged against the door, her cheerful expression belying the pretended exhaustion. "I guess it's a preview of Doctors Circle next May."

"In what way?" Patrick collected stray wrappers that seemed to have appeared by magic, perhaps because he and Natalie had been helping themselves to the treats.

"Think how many babies are due in May! In addition to ours, Heather's nurse is having twins and Loretta's sister is scheduled to deliver triplets.'' She patted her rounded abdomen. ''It's a population explosion.''

''So it is.'' After tossing aside his mask and cat ears, Patrick gathered her close. ''Can I mess up your makeup now?''

Natalie burrowed into him, all soft fur and feminine curves. ''We can start in the front hall. Then which room would you like to explore?''

''All of them,'' he said.

She gave a happy sigh. ''It's nice to be home.''

LATER, LYING UPSTAIRS beside her friend and lover, Natalie remembered her words and recognized the truth in them. This was her home now, hers and Patrick's.

He'd meant what he said about sharing it equally. Maybe his willingness to offend Chief Sorrell might seem like a small thing to others, but not to her.

Suddenly she couldn't wait to move in. In the quiet warmth of the king-size bed, in the house where she and her husband would spend the rest of their lives, she felt utterly safe and utterly loved.

It was the best feeling in the world.

* * * * *

*Don't miss the next book
in Jacqueline Diamond's*
THE BABIES OF DOCTORS CIRCLE *series!*
Look for
*PRESCRIPTION: MARRY HER
IMMEDIATELY,*
*coming in May 2003
from Harlequin American Romance.*

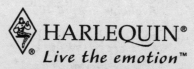

**A "Mother of the Year" contest brings
overwhelming response as thousands of women
vie for the luxurious grand prize....**

Kate Hoffmann

Jacqueline Diamond

Jill Shalvis

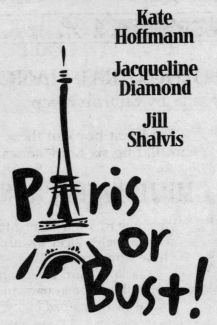

Paris or Bust!

A hilarious and romantic trio of new stories!

With a trip to Paris at stake, these women are
determined to win! But the laughs are many as three of
them discover that being finalists isn't the most
excitement they'll ever have.... Falling in love is!

Available in April 2003.

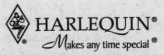

HARLEQUIN®
Makes any time special®

If you enjoyed what you just read,
then we've got an offer you can't resist!

Take 2 bestselling
love stories FREE!
Plus get a FREE surprise gift!

Clip this page and mail it to Harlequin Reader Service®

IN U.S.A.	IN CANADA
3010 Walden Ave.	P.O. Box 609
P.O. Box 1867	Fort Erie, Ontario
Buffalo, N.Y. 14240-1867	L2A 5X3

YES! Please send me 2 free Harlequin American Romance® novels and my free surprise gift. After receiving them, if I don't wish to receive anymore, I can return the shipping statement marked cancel. If I don't cancel, I will receive 4 brand-new novels every month, before they're available in stores! In the U.S.A., bill me at the bargain price of $3.99 plus 25¢ shipping & handling per book and applicable sales tax, if any*. In Canada, bill me at the bargain price of $4.74 plus 25¢ shipping & handling per book and applicable taxes**. That's the complete price and a savings of at least 10% off the cover prices—what a great deal! I understand that accepting the 2 free books and gift places me under no obligation ever to buy any books. I can always return a shipment and cancel at any time. Even if I never buy another book from Harlequin, the 2 free books and gift are mine to keep forever.

154 HDN DNT7
354 HDN DNT9

Name	(PLEASE PRINT)	
Address	Apt.#	
City	State/Prov.	Zip/Postal Code

* Terms and prices subject to change without notice. Sales tax applicable in N.Y.
** Canadian residents will be charged applicable provincial taxes and GST.
  All orders subject to approval. Offer limited to one per household and not valid to
  current Harlequin American Romance® subscribers.
  ® are registered trademarks of Harlequin Enterprises Limited.

AMER02   ©2001 Harlequin Enterprises Limited

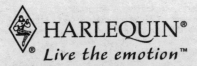

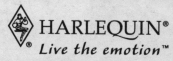

C O O P E R ' S  C O R N E R

Welcome to Cooper's Corner...
a small town with very big surprises!

Coming in April 2003...
JUST ONE LOOK
by Joanna Wayne

Check-in: After a lifetime of teasing, Cooper's Corner postmistress Alison Fairchild finally had the cutest nose ever—thanks to recent plastic surgery! At her friend's wedding, all eyes were on her, except those of the gorgeous stranger in the dark glasses—then she realized he was blind.

Checkout: Ethan Granger wasn't the sightless teacher everyone thought, but an undercover FBI agent. When he met Alison, he was thankful for those dark glasses. If she could see into his eyes, she'd know he was in love....

HARLEQUIN®
Makes any time special ®

CC-CNM9

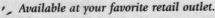
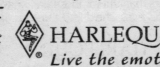
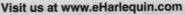